UN-FUR-TUNATE MURDERS

A Wonder Cats Mystery Book 6

HARPER LIN

ISBN-13: 978-1987859461

ISBN-10: 1987859464

www.harperlin.com

CONTENTS

Two Bright Dots

✤✤✤

"I love thunderstorms," I mused as I stared out the window of the café. "There is something soothing about them. Even with the thunder and the lightning. If it could rain every day, all day, I wouldn't mind at all."

The sky had started to gray over almost immediately after the sun rose. By noon, it was the color of a tombstone. By three o'clock, there were little drops darkening the sidewalk. But now, at seven in the evening, our town of Wonder Falls was going through a thorough cleansing.

Since the Brew-Ha-Ha Café was my home away from home, and the owner was my aunt Astrid, and my coworker was my cousin and best bud Bea, I could have stood in the window all night, listening to the thunder and pounding drops of rain.

"Rain makes me sleepy," Aunt Astrid stated just before a yawn stretched her mouth wide open. She lazily shuffled her tarot cards like a blackjack dealer in Las Vegas. "This is good sleeping weather."

"What?" Bea interrupted as she nervously folded napkins and plastic utensils together in preparation for tomorrow's morning rush. "This is 'run home and get the flashlights, the shortwave radio, and bottled water ready in case the power goes out' weather. That's what this is."

"Are you kidding?" I looked at my cousin as if she had just started to speak fluent Swahili. "I've seen you eat kale. Raw. There is nothing more terrifying than that. But a little thunder and lightning makes you nervous."

Bea stuck her tongue out at me.

"This is slow, slow, slow." Aunt Astrid made a fan out of her cards then slapped them all back into a brick. "We haven't had this slow a night in a long time."

The rain was really coming down now in sheets. I walked over to the light switch and lowered the dimmer just a little so it was still obvious we were open, but it threw a warm glow out the windows at the storm clouds. The candles on the tables flickered happily and, although I hated to admit it, made the whole place look terribly romantic.

The smell of coffee still lingered, as we had made fresh pots of both regular and decaf as well as hot water for tea. There were bound to be one or two stragglers who didn't pay attention to the forecast, right? The evening's desserts, including a triple-layer chocolate cake and a fabulous apple pie, were tempting me from the display case.

"Those desserts aren't going to keep until tomorrow." I let my eyes bounce quickly from Aunt Astrid to Bea then immediately to the chocolate cake. "I'll share a slice with you."

"Deal." Bea pulled out a dainty little saucer with blue flowers around the rim and two forks.

"How's this?" I measured a slice about two inches thick. Bea looked at her mother, who was paying no attention to us, and then quickly nodded. With a smile and my tongue already licking the corners of my mouth, I cut a huge wedge of cake, took a plate, slapped it on there, and quickly closed the dessert case.

With a fork, I gouged myself a mouthful, shoveling it in as if I hadn't eaten for a week.

"I don't know what you did with this one, Bea,

but it is the best chocolate cake I've ever tasted in my life," I mumbled, careful not to let a single crumb fall from my mouth.

"Talk to Kevin. He suggested adding this fancy cocoa he found in Germany. It costs a little more, but I think he only added an extra teaspoon, and it has made all the difference." Bea took a giant bite.

"Well, I will tell him tomorrow."

Kevin was our baker. He had been with us since we rebuilt the cafe after the fire, and although he was a man of few words, his baking was a feast for every one of the senses.

Kevin had probably made it safely home before all the rain started. As usual, he left the door open and the back screen closed, helping to cool off the kitchen and get fresh air throughout the place. It also allowed for a special visitor to come and go as he liked.

"*Meow.*"

"Treacle!" I turned and saw my beautiful black feline companion looking ten pounds lighter, with his fur sticking tightly to his body. He was soaked to the skin.

"*What have you been doing out in that mess?*" I asked him telepathically.

I set my fork down and grabbed a towel to wrap

around him. Vigorously, I rubbed him behind the ears, making his purr machine kick in. *"I thought cats hated getting wet."*

"We do."

He pulled off the towel and shook, sending tiny droplets all over the floor and me. I continued to rub his fur until he was a good bit dryer. Then, scooping him in my arms, I placed him on the window ledge. Without concern, he began to groom himself.

"Is there anything going on out there that I should know about?" My question made Treacle snap an ear in my direction.

"There is a lot of electricity in the air. I thought I could smell something coming but couldn't be sure," he replied without looking at me.

"Something good or something bad?"

Treacle looked up and narrowed his jade eyes at me.

"I don't know."

I scratched his back. With each stroke, I received an affectionate head-butt. When I turned to go back to my cake, all I saw was an empty plate and Bea licking her fork.

"Hey!" I stomped over to my cousin with my hands on my hips. "You greedy hog. Cut me another piece."

"If I do that, we won't have enough to give to the guys working the late shift at the police station." Bea giggled.

"You wolfed that down like a pug does a slice of bacon. You should really be ashamed of yourself," I teased. "And don't tell me you're giving that to the cops. Just because your husband's working tonight doesn't mean you can steal that cake out of my mouth and give it to him. Give him the kale."

Bea's shoulders were shaking uncontrollably as she tried not to laugh out loud.

"Aunt Astrid didn't raise you to be such a miser," I kept rambling, the decadent taste of the chocolate cake slowly disintegrating in my mouth. I looked out the window. "I don't know how you'll get to sleep tonight, knowing this is how you treat your cousin."

"I'll manage." Bea chuckled. "I think I better start wrapping this stuff up for Jake and the guys at the station."

I clicked my tongue and shook my head. Bea's husband, Jake, was a detective at the Wonder Falls Police Station. When there were leftovers from the café, we boxed them up, and Bea made a special delivery to the guys. It was also an excuse for her and Jake to gaze into each other's eyes and play kissy face for a little while. They were still so in love it was almost sickening.

Going back to the window, I looked out and watched the blinking lightning in the distance.

"I think it's supposed to continue raining all night. Maybe not this hard, but we're supposed to have another gray day tomorrow." I rocked on my heels. I wasn't sure what it was about this kind of weather, but I always liked gloomy days. "We probably won't have too many customers tomorrow, either." I shrugged and looked at Treacle, who had stretched out. The tip of his tail was the only part moving.

"That will be too bad," Bea replied. "Kevin and I had planned for a fantastic melted-brie and kale sandwich with a touch of sliced apple and some special seasoning we concocted together that we both agreed would be delicious on soft homemade French bread."

"Kale again?" I said, wrinkling my nose.

"Would you rather I use spinach?" she asked thoughtfully.

"I'd rather you make cheeseburgers."

"I don't think we are going to get any more customers tonight." Aunt Astrid yawned again. "We might as well close up early." She pushed herself up from her seat, neatly stacked her tarot cards, and placed them in a beautiful wooden box that she then slipped into a dark-purple velvet drawstring bag. But before she could return them to their special shelf in the back of the café where she normally did her readings, she stopped in her tracks and pointed at the window.

I turned and looked where she was pointing.

They started off as just two bright dots down the street. But coming to us faster than normal, the approaching headlights became bigger and bigger.

Without thinking, I quickly scooped Treacle up in my arms and backed up several paces as Aunt Astrid joined Bea behind the counter. For a second, we all thought the car was going to burst through the storefront windows. But we heard the sound of the brakes. The car jerked as it came to a stop, the wheels screeching and the shocks groaning.

All three of us just stared, our mouths slack and our eyes wide.

Within seconds, the car engine was off, the lights out, and the driver frantically popping out of the driver's seat, slamming the door shut. With her head down against the pouring rain, she raced to our entrance. The little wind-chime bells went off as she yanked the door open.

County Line Road 63

⚜

"Thank God you're still open!" the woman cried.

"Tamara Watson? Is that you underneath all that wet hair?" Aunt Astrid asked, suddenly alert and wide awake.

I felt Treacle go rigid in my arms. His back began to arch, every hair on his body puffing him out to twice his normal size. His green eyes widened.

"What's gotten into you?" I asked with my mind.

"She's sick." With a gravelly growl, Treacle leapt from my arms and headed out the back door back into the rain without uttering a word. I turned to our new guest.

"Yes." Tamara pulled her long, black, soaking-wet hair away from her face and tried to smile. "It's me."

"My heavens, dear. Are you all right?" Aunt Astrid quickly grabbed a clean white towel from behind the counter and handed it over to the girl.

"Bea, get her a tea," I suggested as I pulled out a chair for her to sit down. Her entire body looked like a blur. She was trembling, maybe a little from the cold and a little from something else.

Tamara Watson was one of our regular customers. Aunt Astrid consulted the tarot cards for her on a monthly basis, and we also knew her from around town. She was a single girl, working as a secretary of an accounting firm.

None of us had ever seen her in such a state, nor had we ever seen anyone as pale. At least, not someone who still had a pulse.

I looked to Bea, who was busy with her back to us, her arms flying in a graceful display as she reached for her ingredients, ground them together, placed them in a tea steeper, and dropped the steeper into one of our large to-go cups.

While pouring the hot water over the steeper, Bea looked at me and shrugged. I looked from Bea to Tamara and back to Bea again.

"Your tea will be ready in a second, Tamara. Just sit tight." Bea watched her mom take a seat next to the shaken woman. We all noticed Tamara would not stop looking at the floor.

"Honey," Aunt Astrid said soothingly as she sat down next to her. "Are you in trouble?"

Call me cynical, but my first thought was she hit someone on the road. A car broke down. The driver got out to walk to a gas station. Visibility was bad, and *whammo*! She was too shocked, too scared, too freaked out to stop. That was all I could think of that would cause someone to be so terrified. Tamara wasn't a hit-and-run kind of person. She was a normal person in an abnormal situation. At least that was what I was thinking when she began to speak.

"She came out of nowhere."

I knew it.

"Who did, honey?" Aunt Astrid said soothingly.

"I was coming down Route 41 on my way to my sister's house. She lives in Muncee." Tamara took the towel my aunt had handed her and wiped her face. Some of her makeup smeared. She still looked at the floor.

"She called me on my cell and said that her mother-in-law had just heard on her police scanner that there was an accident on Torrence Avenue. Traffic was all backed up, and nothing was coming or going."

We all watched her take a deep breath, but her eyes still hadn't climbed higher than her own feet on the floor.

Bea brought the honey-colored tea over to Tamara and set it on the table. No sooner had she done that than Tamara wrapped her cold hands around the warm cardboard cup.

"I said no big deal. I'd go around. If I overshot to the next exit, I knew there'd be a way to backtrack. It might be a little out of the way, but I was in no hurry. So I went past Torrence and got off at Bourbonnais. I took that down a ways and turned on County Line Road 63."

She brought the cup to her lips, took a sip, and wrinkled her nose.

"I was the only one out there. At first, I saw the corn rows on each side of me, but they gave way to what looked like forest preserve or just a more wild stretch of land. There were trees and bushes and things on either side of the road. But there was no life but me."

She swallowed hard.

"I thought it was just on account of the weather being so lousy. That's what I told myself. Only a lunatic would be out here driving in this weather." Tamara chuckled bitterly. "But I couldn't shake the feeling that I was driving in a bubble. Every sound seemed muffled. The lights lit up the road ahead, but I couldn't help but wonder. What was just ahead of them? What was staying just out of sight? I was alone. I wouldn't see anyone else, and no one else would see me. But something did see me."

"Some *thing*?" I asked.

"There was something on that road." Tamara took another sip of tea but made a face again as if she had just swallowed vinegar or maybe a spoonful of castor oil. It wasn't like Bea to screw up one of her concoctions, so when I looked to her, I was surprised to see her studying Tamara's reactions.

"What did you see out there, honey?" Aunt Astrid asked gently.

Tamara's chin began to quiver, and she licked her lips nervously.

"At first, I thought it was a white trash bag that had gotten stuck in a tree. It was whipping around in and out of the high beams as I drove closer. Just a sack caught in some branches, I kept thinking. But then I realized it was moving toward me."

"What was?" I asked.

Tamara took a deep breath, and her eyes filled with tears.

"It wasn't stuck in branches or bushes. It was on the side of the road, and it was hobbling toward me."

"Hobbling?"

Tamara looked right at me as if she were pleading for me to fix it, come up with answers for a question she hadn't asked yet.

"I don't know how to describe it," she whispered as if saying anything too loudly might cause whatever she saw to appear right in the middle of the Brew-Ha-Ha Café. "I think it was a person. Or maybe it was a person at one time. It was in an accident, or it was deformed or something. The shoulders were up so high that it looked like the head was coming from the middle of where the chest would be. The hands and arms were curled over onto themselves like claws, like the front legs of a praying mantis. I thought I saw feet, but something made me think they were..." Her voice trailed off. Squeezing her eyelids together, she obviously didn't want to say any more.

"Think they were what?" Aunt Astrid's voice was firm.

"Hooves." Tamara's voice was low. "I thought maybe someone was playing a joke. This was a prank or one of those schemes where gangbangers or rapists try to set something up to get a person to stop or get out of their car on a lonely road so they can rob you, or worse."

I watched as Tamara's trembling hands made another grab for the tea. To me, it smelled delicious. But Tamara brought it to her nose and, without another sip, placed it at the very opposite edge of the table.

"I didn't slow down. But I didn't speed up, either. As I got closer, I saw its head was twisted unnaturally to one side, almost like it was upside down. The chin was pushed into the arched shoulder on the right side. How could a person live like that? How could they stand or walk, let alone stomp after someone in a downpour?"

She looked to all of us for answers that we didn't have.

"And with only half of its face exposed, how could it see me? Because it did! It stared at me with one eye that looked milky with cataracts! Almost pure white compared to the sickly color of the skin, which reminded me of the underside of a frog! Pale, greenish, and almost translucent!"

Aunt Astrid took Tamara's hands in hers. It calmed her enough so she could continue.

"I hit the gas, but my tires wouldn't grip on the slick pavement. The wheels spun and spun, and I barely moved an inch. Meanwhile, that thing was getting closer." Tamara's body began to shake. "I didn't want to, but I had to ease up off the gas so the tires could grab the road. When I did that, it was like a flash, and the thing was directly in front of my car! I honked the horn! But it wouldn't get out of the way!"

Tamara pulled her hands away from Aunt Astrid's and covered her eyes. This was where I was sure she was going to say she accelerated and drove right over the person, thing, whatever it was. But I was wrong.

"I put the car in reverse and began backing away from the thing. I watched it for a second then turned around to watch where I was driving, and it appeared behind me, clomping and hobbling at a furious pace to keep up. It had to be a second one, right?"

Not that a second cloven-hooved hunchback in a white sack with its head on backward was in any way more comforting. I kept this thought to myself.

"I slammed on the brakes. The entire car lurched. I couldn't tell if the pounding I was hearing was the rain or my own heart or the sound of those hooves shaking the ground. When I spun around, there was nothing in front of me but the headlights and the pavement. I looked in the rearview mirror and turned my head to look out the back, and nothing was there either."

"So you hit the gas and got out of dodge?" I asked.

"I was about to." Tamara looked up at me with a pitiful smile on her face. "But as I went to shift from reverse to drive, I felt it. Before I saw it at the driver's-side window, I felt its eye staring at me. Into me. It was grinning insanely, staring in at me before it started to claw at the window. Like a dog digging in dirt, it scraped its hands and nails furiously at the glass."

Bea gasped. Aunt Astrid leaned back in her chair. I just stood there like a dolt.

She put her hands up to her ears. "It kept asking me to let it in. In a child's voice, it kept asking me to let it in. Then it stopped. It was like it just noticed there was a handle for the door. It stared at me and then at the handle and then at me again as it reached its deformed hand out then licked its lips with a black tongue. I screamed."

"Yes, I'd say that was the proper response," I mumbled.

Tamara managed to let out a tiny chuckle then shook her head.

"I hit the gas and tore out of there as fast as I

could." She was panting slightly, as if retelling the whole incident included sprinting for five hundred yards. "I forgot about going to my sister's. I got back on the expressway and wanted to get somewhere, anywhere where there were people. You guys were the only place lit up and open." She wiped her eyes and looked at the tea on the table. "I'm sorry, Bea. I don't know what you put in it, but I can't drink it."

"That's okay, Tamara." Bea looked at her mother, who gave her a knowing glance back. I could sense something was wrong, but my specialty was talking to animals, and Treacle had left. He knew something was up and skedaddled. So I watched my cousin and aunt closely.

"You just rest for a few minutes, honey." Aunt Astrid patted Tamara's hands. "I think you are in shock."

"You don't believe me, do you?" Tamara whined as she rubbed her stomach.

"On the contrary. I do believe you. I believe there are things on this planet that are here to help us, and there are definitely things here to do us harm." Aunt Astrid pushed herself up from her seat. "Angels. Devils. Creatures we don't understand. Monsters we don't want to. But none of that changes the fact that we are human and sometimes need help from other places."

"I don't know what you put in that tea, Bea, but it isn't agreeing with me at all." Tamara winced.

"That's okay. I just thought it might help calm your nerves."

"By calming do you mean make it feel like there is a snake writhing around in my gut?"

"No. That would be her lentil meatloaf." I couldn't help myself. When an opportunity like that presents itself, I have to take it, no matter how inappropriate.

"I'm serious." Tamara clutched her stomach. "I don't like this."

Aunt Astrid quickly went to her back table where she usually did her tarot readings and grabbed a small basket full of what looked like trinkets.

"Tamara, honey, hold one of these in each hand." My aunt gave her two smooth stones of pale-pink quartz. They were especially helpful with an upset stomach.

"Maybe I should just get home," Tamara protested.

"You're in no condition to drive." Bea put her hand on Tamara's shoulder but pulled it back as if she were scalding hot. Like I could talk to the animals telepathically, Bea was sort of an empath. She could see into a person's aura and, like a doctor looking at an x-ray, could pinpoint the problem and hopefully do something to alleviate or even remove the trouble.

I could tell by the look on Bea's face she felt something was very wrong with Tamara.

"I'm feeling much better," Tamara lied. "I think I just need to get home and lie down. I still haven't even called my sister."

"Why don't you call her from here, tell her..." My aunt looked up at the ceiling. "Tell her you aren't feeling well and had to pull over and will be going home soon."

Tamara looked at Aunt Astrid. My aunt was a kind person, and it radiated from her, in her flowing blouses, long, graying hair, and her crystal-blue eyes. There was confidence there that a person couldn't help but rest in, and from the look on Tamara's face, she desperately needed to.

Suddenly, the poor girl began to weep.

Psychic Assistance

✦✦✦

"What's the matter with me?" she sobbed pitifully, clenching her teeth as well as the pink stones in her hands.

"You've had a horrible shock, honey." Aunt Astrid was firm in her diagnosis, like a doctor giving bad news but insisting there was hope. "Now, just listen to my voice. You are with friends in a safe place." She pulled the little table away from Tamara and stood in front of her.

"Cath, lock the front door and draw the blinds," Aunt Astrid ordered. "Bea, bring me some sage, my bowl, and a book of matches."

Both of us did as we were told. The rain still

pounded mercilessly outside, but inside the café, it was warm and calm, for the moment.

I shut off the lights, leaving just the candles on the table to give everything a warm, golden glow.

"I knew something was wrong with her when she wouldn't drink the tea," Bea whispered to me as she scooted past me to get the supplies her mother had asked for. "It had a few healing leaves in it. Mint. Chamomile. A few other things. It's very sweet. But she wouldn't touch it."

Aunt Astrid nodded after hearing what Bea had said. She continued talking to Tamara in a low voice, and it was just a matter of minutes before Tamara was relaxed, her eyes drowsy slits and her breathing deep and calm.

Bea returned from the back of the café with everything her mother had requested.

Aunt Astrid took the sage, crumbled up some of it, and placed it in the little brass bowl that was "Aunt Astrid's Bowl." She had gotten it from a shaman friend of hers from New Mexico many years ago. Every year, she got a Christmas card from the fellow, but Bea and I had never met him. I always envisioned a dark-skinned man with jet-black hair that stretched down his entire back and was gray at the temples, and was wrapped in pelts. He was probably just some dude who wore blue jeans and flannel shirts, but I preferred the exotic qualities my imagination provided.

The burning sage wafted in perfect smoky tendrils up into the air. Aunt Astrid was mumbling a few things, but I couldn't make out the words. Then, suddenly, Tamara started to talk. But it wasn't her. Her mouth snapped open and shut like a ventriloquist's dummy. Words came out, but her throat didn't produce them.

They were nonsense words, things a child might say, babblings and ramblings that might have been a spiritual language or maybe just something messing with us.

Whatever it was, it was freaking me out. I took Bea's hand, and she squeezed mine in return. It was good to know she was terrified out of her skin as well. Misery loves company.

"…in the field where it lives. See the bottom. See the top. Let me in. Let me in. Let me in…"

Aunt Astrid spoke so quietly I couldn't hear her at all. But her eyes were focused sharply on Tamara, whose jaw kept moving, but her lips didn't match the sounds coming out.

"Bea, I need you to take the parasite from her stomach," Aunt Astrid commanded.

"Oh no." I groaned. "Astral spiders? I should have known. The poor girl. Hang on, Tamara. You'll make it, girl."

Having recently suffered a bout with astral spiders, I knew a thing or two about how they operate. First, they are spiders. Gross enough, I know. But they feed off your energy and make you depressed and exhausted and ultimately can lead to madness or even suicide.

When I had them, I was as depressed as any teenager on the planet. It was miserable. And the buggers were sunk in so deep on me that Aunt Astrid and Bea both had to yank the suckers free. It was as if I were some kind of buffet, all you can eat.

"No. Not astral spiders. This is more like a tapeworm," my aunt replied.

"Eww."

"Yeah, and it's about the size of a ferret. Plus, it has a human face."

"What?" I hissed.

"Cath, I need you to hold Tamara by her shoulders." Aunt Astrid's voice was calm but firm. She was tightly holding Tamara's hands as Tamara continued to babble in the freakish childlike voice that wasn't her own. "Do it now."

Quickly, I went behind Tamara and put my hands on her shoulders and held her down. She wasn't so much fighting me as she was twitching and jerking in strange spasms.

Bea rubbed her hands together and studied Tamara's body. I could see her eyes searching for something. Her face relaxed when she zeroed in on the spot where the parasite was. With the precision and speed of a cobra, she lunged forward and placed her hands on Tamara's stomach.

Tamara's head swiveled and rotated like a bobblehead stuck to the dashboard of a jeep driving on a dirt path through the woods.

"Have you got it?" Aunt Astrid asked

"Almost." Bea grunted. Her hands were trembling. Her movements made it look as if she were treading water or pushing covers aside until her eyes jumped wide open and she bit her lower lip.

"There you are." She gritted her teeth. Aunt Astrid began to chant in a low and whispery voice. Bea braced one leg in front of her and the other behind her. As if she were in a tug-of-war game, she used her body to pull at the thing.

Tamara's skin was getting hotter by the second.

Finally, Bea had loosened whatever it was. As she pulled back, I saw what she was wrestling with.

Aunt Astrid was right. It was about as wide as a ferret, but it was a sickly white, almost translucent thing with a hideous head and face. A pointy tongue darted in and out of its mouth, and its eyes rolled up into its head.

Bea wouldn't let it go. As she yanked and pulled at the creature, finally getting it almost all the way out of Tamara's belly, Aunt Astrid blew the smoke of the sage into the creature's face and began to mutter a binding spell to send the thing back to where it came from.

In a gross display, its skin split open, just like a real snake's, and it writhed and wiggled itself out of Bea's hands, screaming in a childlike voice.

"You don't belong here!" Aunt Astrid shouted. "Go back where you came from, or forever be imprisoned in this dimension as a monster to be tortured, leered at, and hated."

She moved the bowl of smoldering sage underneath the thing until it dissolved into the air. Bea was left holding an empty sheath of skin. Before she could move, it turned black, shriveled up, and disappeared.

"Is it dead?" I asked. "Did you kill it?"

I looked at Bea, who pulled her hands back to reveal they were now also black, as though she had been handling bricks of coal.

"It's not dead." Aunt Astrid slowly began to bring Tamara out of her trance. "It just shed its skin and went back to where it came from." She studied Tamara, who already had a healthier color to her cheeks. "Tamara, I want you to listen to me. Everything is okay now. You don't have any pain. Your fright was due to the weather."

Tamara started to blink, and her eyes became wide and alert.

"What happened?" Tamara looked around nervously as if she were concerned that we took her wallet or snapshots of her while she was asleep.

"You just needed a little psychic assistance," Aunt Astrid offered as I scooted back around the counter to check Bea as she washed her hands. I saw she had a few blisters on the palm by her thumb. Other than that, she was okay.

"Are you feeling better?" Bea asked over her shoulder.

"Yes." Tamara rubbed her stomach but did it more out of habit than anything else. "Bea, can you make one of your famous detox teas for me? With all this rain and goofy driving, I think I could use something to help clear out the system." She chuckled.

When Tamara was getting ready to leave, she wasn't sure she had seen exactly what she thought she had seen on County Line Road 63.

"It was like a tsunami had hit out there." She shook her head. "I don't really know what I saw, but it was pretty wild. It was probably just some dorks out there trying a prank on the first car to come by in months. But either way, I think I'll call my sister and tell her I'll come by next weekend when the weather is better."

"Well, you're all right now, and the next time you're driving and you see Big Foot or the Slender-man, give us a shout," I teased, handing her the large tea that Bea had prepared for her. All of us waved it off as being on the house, making Tamara smile even more, and she promised to stop in again soon for a tarot reading.

"That was a weird one," Bea said.

I watched through the slits in the blinds as Tamara ran for her car, climbed in, revved it up, and pulled away. She drove off as if it were just another rainy night and she was out getting some tea.

"Yeah," I concurred. "How about I give everyone a lift home tonight? No need to walk in this rain if you can help it. An umbrella won't do you any good."

"Have you cleaned out the backseat yet? I would rather not sit waist deep in empty fast food bags." Bea knew my weakness was a good greasy burger from just about any fast food place.

"Well, if you'd rather walk," I teased.

After closing the café for the night, we all piled into my beater and headed for home. First, we dropped off Bea, who lived just three doors down from my aunt, who lived almost directly across the street from me. If you were to look at our houses from space, the distance made an almost perfect triangle.

Once I was inside my house, I went directly to the kitchen and saw my favorite green eyes staring at me from the kitchen window.

"Well, you sure took off in a hurry," I scolded Treacle as I opened the window for him to slink in like a wet, furry specter.

"I didn't like the shift in the mojo in there," he said. I grabbed a towel and proceeded to conduct our drying ritual all over again, starting with the top of his head and working my way down to the base of his tail. He shook his fur wildly then proceeded to lick his legs and tail, stopping to watch me as I opened the fridge

for a glass of milk. *"There was something wrong with that woman."*

"Yes," I answered telepathically. *"You're lucky you missed it. It was pretty gross."* I wrinkled my nose. *"I was going to burn some candles and enjoy the light show from the bedroom. You ready to relax?"*

"I think you may want to wash up first."

I looked at my hands and the front of my shirt. Sure, I knew I wasn't as neat as Bea was, but I didn't think I had gotten dirty at work. I quickly sniffed my armpit but detected no offensive odor.

"What's the matter?"

He focused his eyes on my stomach. I looked down and only saw the fabric of my black T-shirt. But as I watched Treacle, his tail began to whip back and forth.

Now, as I mentioned before, I had a bout with astral spiders, and I wasn't about to go through that again. So I quickly grabbed a wad of dried sage, my white candles that happened to smell like fresh linen, and some salt and performed a quick purification spell.

Once all the sage was burned and the candles were burnt out, I sat down on the edge of my bed and looked at Treacle.

"Are we good? Do you see anything else? Do I need to

call Aunt Astrid? Please tell me you don't see any astral spiders."

"*I didn't see any of those to begin with.*" He hopped up on my lap, his motor purring loudly. "*I just thought something might have been trying to stow away on you. But I don't sense it now.*" He walked around on my lap, making three circles, until he finally snuggled down.

I wanted to get comfortable myself. I looked down at the big bundle of fur in my lap. He looked up at me and made no attempt to move. So I scooped him up like a baby in my arms, went into my small living room, and took a seat in my comfy chair facing the window that faced my tiny backyard. The rain fell in a steady rhythm, and the lightning flashed.

While I stroked Treacle's fur and enjoyed the soothing sound, I gave very little thought to what had happened at the café. Maybe I was too tired to focus, or maybe I just chalked it up as one of those weird examples of nature's mysteries. I don't know. But within a few minutes, Treacle and I were both sound asleep, and I kept rerunning the same odd dream.

There was a collapsed bridge, and I was digging through the rubble with my bare hands. They were dirty and bloody from pulling at rocks, but just as I was inches away from reaching what I was digging for, I'd wake up, only to return there again.

When I woke up, I didn't really think about it as it faded quickly, as dreams usually do. That was, until Bea arrived at work.

Pectus Adsecula

❧⚜❧

"So let me take a head count. One. Two. Great. Everyone survived the storm," Aunt Astrid joked as Bea let herself in the back door of the café. "I slept like a log and feel refreshed. Even on this brisk November morning, I feel all warm inside."

"Survived the storm? Just barely." Bea sighed. "I had the shortwave radio on most of the night in case a tornado touched down. I didn't want to risk sleeping through the Wonder Falls emergency siren."

"Did you keep poor Jake up, too?" I asked. Jake, Bea's husband, was a real trooper to put up with some of Bea's quirks, like her vegan cooking and her health-conscious habits, not to mention the fact she was a witch, and so were the rest of us Greenstones.

"He had no choice." Bea raised her eyebrows. "Who else was I going to talk to? Peanut Butter just kept snuggling closer and closer to me every time the thunder rumbled. Poor thing was a nervous wreck."

I felt bad about that. Peanut Butter, Bea's feline companion, was still just a baby compared to Aunt Astrid's gigantic Maine Coon cat, Marshmallow, and my Treacle, who was a beautiful black alley cat, a rebel. Not much made him nervous, but when he got spooked, as he did yesterday, you can bet I paid attention.

"So either of you guys know what that was that *literally* got into Tamara yesterday?"

"The technical name for it is *pectus adsecula*. A soul parasite," Aunt Astrid said while opening the blinds and letting the sun shine into the café.

"That's even grosser than the description you gave last night." I balked. "Bea, you got anything you can whip up for a queasy stomach? This is really too much."

With wide eyes, Bea nodded and said she'd be making enough for the two of us. Aunt Astrid didn't seem fazed.

"The funny thing is those creatures are usually only picked up if a person is passing through a mass of decomposing material."

Aunt Astrid pursed her lips and put her hand on her hip. She stared into the space in front of her, as she did often.

With the gift of being able to see multiple dimensions within this one, she was never just daydreaming but rather scanning the layers of realms that coexisted all together yet separately.

"Not dead things like we're used to here. But rather those dead and dying things that are otherworldly. Take, for example, a cemetery. They're loaded with this kind of energy. But because it is sacred ground and has been blessed, this type of decomposition doesn't occur. People can go and visit their loved ones and emerge without any residue or contamination." Aunt Astrid's face became grave. "But take the Killing Fields in Cambodia or Dachau in Germany, or any place where mass graves have been found, where evil placed them there, you'll find this kind of creature and even worse sometimes, writhing about in the ethereal debris."

I put my hand to my chest.

"So those souls are just trapped there, rotting like that?"

"Not the souls of *all* the dead. Most move on. But there are always those seeking revenge. Those that were also evil in life may choose to remain there.

Until that evil is unearthed, as it was in both those examples, these kinds of parasites and the creatures make it their home."

"I can understand a place like Dachau." Bea squinted at her mom then handed me a medium paper cup filled with the sweetest-smelling concoction yet. Quickly, I took a sip, and it instantly relieved my churning stomach. "But I don't think there was ever a mass killing in Wonder Falls where a bunch of bodies were dumped."

Aunt Astrid shrugged.

"I've never heard of anything either. But maybe someone should check out that route to Bourbonnais and see what there is to see," I suggested. "Anyone up for a road trip later?"

AFTER A CLOSING THE CAFE, IT DIDN'T TAKE long for Bea and me to load up my car with a couple of flashlights, our heavier coats since the temperature was dropping way down at night this time of year, and some black onyx stones for protection against evil entities of numerous variations. Aunt Astrid also rustled up a quick protection spell that we had hoped would do the trick.

"So Tamara said she was heading to Bourbonnais and took County Line Road 63. I can honestly say that I don't think I've ever taken this road in my whole life. Can that be possible?" Bea asked as I drove.

"I don't see why not. Wonder Falls is a big place, and a good portion of it is wild forest. Who knows what country roads are winding around and through all that we don't know about?" I was talking to hear myself make noise. Truthfully, I was starting to get a little anxious.

We drove down the same route Tamara said she took and found the exit for the county line road. Surprisingly, it was a paved road. For some reason, I had envisioned a dirt road with manhole-sized potholes and craggily barren trees bowing down overhead.

"Well, this doesn't look too bad," Bea said, to which I nodded.

"Looks like a regular road to me." I drove about twenty-five miles an hour as we both looked out the windows, searching for anything that looked like a mass grave. Needless to say we saw nothing of the sort.

"What do you say we stop and walk around a bit?" Bea suggested. The more I drove, the more I was beginning to think that Tamara might have just had some kind of episode, driving in such bad weather. Perhaps she had a waking nightmare or even a hallucination.

"I think that's fine with me." I slowed the car down and pulled over on the side of the road.

I snapped my hazard lights on to make sure no one coming down this isolated road at seventy miles an hour would plow into my car. I left the headlights on and climbed out. Bea had the flashlights and handed one to me. We clicked them on, and with her on one side of the road and me on the other, we began to walk.

"I see bushes." I sighed. "Lots of trees."

"Me, too. And I can see my breath when I talk." She withdrew an adorable red hat with a pom-pom on the top out of her coat pocket and pulled it over her head and ears. I was wearing my hood up and tied tightly around my chin.

"I didn't realize it was supposed to get so cold tonight. Good thing it stopped raining last night, or all of this might freeze," I said, pulling a pair of leather gloves from my pockets and putting them on. The beam of my flashlight shook slightly as I shivered from the cold.

The air smelled like wet grass and cold dirt.

Earthy and sleepy as nature began its long hibernation and winter quickly approached. Technically, it was still fall, but the temperature said otherwise.

"I don't see anything. Do you?" Bea asked, swinging her flashlight in my direction.

"Nope. Don't see anything. Don't hear anything." But just then, I froze. I turned around and shined the flashlight into the bushes. The only sound I heard were my boots scraping on the asphalt. "Bea?"

"Yeah?" She walked over to me, looking bored and let down that there wasn't a repeat of the previous evening's excitement. Her shoes on the road were also loud and the only sound I heard.

"Listen." I held my breath.

"I don't hear anything." She shrugged.

"Right? Not anything?"

She stood still and shined her flashlight around.

I strained to hear anything. Still holding my breath, I tried to hear a bird, the rustle of dry leaves, an airplane flying overhead, a car honking from the expressway, even just a hint of the wind. But there was nothing.

Suddenly, it seemed as if every noise we made was amplified a thousand times.

"What's happened to everything?" Bea whispered, but even her voice sounded so loud I was terrified something would hear us.

"I don't know." I practically just mouthed the words, not wanting to give away where we were to anything that might be out there.

"Do you feel that?" Bea put her hand on my arm.

"Feel what?"

"Like we're being watched." Bea's lips and eyes were the only things that moved as she held her flashlight in one direction. I didn't dare move, but yes, I, too, suddenly felt as though we were being watched. And not by just one pair of eyes.

The trees, the bushes, the stones, the dirt, the grass, the leaves—everything was watching us. Everything around us seemed to have eyes. They were staring straight at us without blinking, and they were not pleased.

"We should go," Bea hissed.

I didn't need to be told twice. Quickly, with our backs to each other in order to watch from all directions, we got back to the car. For the split second we pulled apart so I could get behind the wheel and Bea could jump into the passenger seat, I was sure we were going to be ambushed by something.

I yanked the door open, jumped in, and slammed the door shut, quickly slapping the lock in place. Bea must have felt the same way, because she was panting after she wrenched her door shut.

With shaky fingers, I turned the car key. The engine roared to life. I threw the vehicle into drive, hit the gas, and whipped the car around to head back in the direction we had come.

"I don't want to go farther in, Bea." I gasped. "I just don't want to see where the road ends. Not tonight. Not at night at all."

"I couldn't agree more." Bea had her hand on the dashboard as if it somehow helped the car move faster.

Once we were back in town, I sped to the Brew-Ha-Ha and parked right in front. When we got out of the car, both Bea and I let out a collective sigh. We could hear birds, the traffic from the next block, and the wind rustling through dried flowers and the leaves in the trees. It was as if we were transported back to civilization.

Bea unlocked the front door, and we stepped in. The café was nice and warm, even though it was closed and the light from our hidden bunker shined into the dining area, letting us know Aunt Astrid was still there.

As we descended the stairs, I smelled something delicious.

"Hey, girls," Aunt Astrid called to us. "Come down here. I've found something neat."

"You have food," I said. "That's exactly what I needed."

"Yes, I've got vegetable soup in the crockpot and some crusty bread. So tell me. Did you guys see anything?"

A shiver ran through my body as I relived the last twenty-five minutes of my life listening to Bea retell it. I ate the warm soup and dunked the bread in the orange tomato broth. There was something magical about soup that could calm the most frazzled nerves.

"We don't even know how to explain it," I added after Bea described how we sped away from County Line Road 63. "There was nothing there, yet something was there, and it was powerful. Sucking all the sound out of the place. What kind of thing does that? No, wait. Don't tell me. I don't want to know. It's probably some gross thing with twelve eyes and the mouth of a great white. If you know what it is, keep it to yourself." I shook my head and shoveled in another hot spoonful of soup.

"I don't know what it could be." Aunt Astrid took her regular seat on the lovely old-fashioned couch she had added to the bunker. We'd discovered this room after the first Brew-Ha-Ha had burned down. It was a great little getaway where Aunt Astrid kept some of her spell books and a supply of wine, water, soda pop, and comfy chairs to sit in even though I always preferred to sit on the floor. It just felt right. "I've never heard of anything like that."

"There is definitely something out there, and it is able to hide when it wants to. When we first got there, we didn't notice anything." Bea filled a small bowl with soup and tore off a chunk of bread. She sat down next to her mother. "We didn't notice anything odd. But we also were looking to see something. I don't know about you, but I don't know if there were sounds when we first got out of the car or not. I couldn't say if things were normal at first and then something scared the entire area into a dead silence. I just don't know."

I tore into the bread with my teeth. Aunt Astrid sat for a moment then grabbed a bowl of soup for herself. After a couple of thoughtful spoonfuls, she spoke.

"We need to find out about that area."

"I'm not going back." I grimaced and shook my head. "Nope. Not without an arsenal of witchy weapons and the bright sun just creeping over the horizon. Nighttime is *not* the right time to visit County Line Road 63."

"I can talk to Jake," Bea offered. "Maybe he knows something."

"That is a good idea." Aunt Astrid nodded then looked at me.

"What?"

"I'm thinking the library might be a good place for you to go." My aunt knew I loved the library. "See if you can find out anything about that part of town on any old maps or if there is anything in the town records."

"That, I can do. The library has lots of people and is only open during the day. I'm good with that."

Evergrave Creek

✿❀✿

Wonder Falls Public Library was a divine old building that looked as if it belonged on a university campus. Its redbrick exterior and wide double doors almost made me feel as though I were entering a royal palace.

The windows and doors were an Art Deco stained-glass design, very symmetrical and very beautiful. When you entered the building, the lobby floor was a green-and-white marble, complemented by the dark oak of the book return and checkout desks. To the right was the children's wing. There was never a time I came to the library when I didn't hear at least two kids talking or laughing or playing in there. Today was no different. But I was heading to the left, the grown-ups' wing, where a massive circular desk in the same dark wood sat stoically in the midst of all the rows and rows of books and desks and computers and magazines.

The woman sitting there was exactly what a librarian was supposed to look like. She was an older lady with black hair pulled back in a bun. Her modern take on horn-rimmed glasses rested on her nose, and a gaudy chain of silver hoops and orange glass beads ensured she wouldn't set them down and forget where they were. Her sweater was buttoned all the way up to her throat on her thin frame.

"Excuse me," I whispered. She turned and smiled up at me, showcasing a huge silver hoop in her left nostril.

"Can I help you?" Her voice was very low and sultry. Another curveball I didn't see coming.

"I'm wondering if the library has some old maps of Wonder Falls or any records of the town and the population over the years that I could take a look at." I smiled.

"Absolutely." She stood up from the desk and only reached a height of about five feet, maybe even less. I followed her through the main area of the library to a small alcove with the words "Donated by

William and Mary Madia" on a bronze commemorative plaque over the door.

"This is our records room." The librarian folded her hands in front of her, grinning excitedly. "We've got newspapers on microfiche that date back to the 1800s if you're just looking for a glimpse at life here when the town was just a baby." She chuckled. "We've also got an extensive database of every transaction of significance that helped build up our lovely town. You can access those on the computers, but it helps to have very, very specific key words. Property purchases, business contracts, census results, yadda, yadda. That's all in there, too. And hanging up like the racks for newspapers are the maps of Wonder Falls from its inception to just three years ago." The woman smiled a huge, toothy grin that nearly made her eyes disappear behind her pushed-up cheeks. "Will this help?"

"This is great," I whispered. "Thanks."

The librarian nodded, and before I could say anything else, she was already walking back the way we had come.

Truthfully, I didn't even know this little section existed. When I came to the library, I usually looked for books to escape reality, like sweet love stories or a fly-by-the-seat-of-my-pants thriller. Aunt Astrid was the history buff, and well, Bea read any nonfiction that had to do with vegan recipes or holistic remedies.

I thought my best bet was to start with the maps. I spread them out and was amazed at how much the town had changed over just the past fifty years.

The area in question around County Line Road 63 was mostly farmland.

"That would explain why it was so quiet out there last night."

I tried to convince myself of that, but nature itself is noisy. If anyone ever ventured out into the woods and just stood still for a second, they'd see what a bustling business nature really was. Squirrels darting in a dozen different directions at once, birds singing, twigs snapping as old ones broke off and died, making room for new buds. At nighttime, it was even more alive with nocturnal hunters—raccoons, opossums, owls, and mice. So that theory quickly went the way of the dodo bird.

As I followed the road on one of the maps from the 1970s, I saw that at one time it had split, one branch following through the farmland for several miles to join with another major road. The other branch wove through the area, crossing a bridge and fairly significant creek that I had never known existed.

That was odd in itself because it is a well-known fact that witches have a unique connection with bodies of water and almost always know where they can be found.

I can recall a few times in the recent past where natural running water saved my hide. The strength of the current or the depth of the bed can have amazing effects on supernatural situations. Not to mention the spirits and mystical creatures that reside there. Sometimes just dipping a toe in the water could mean the difference between life and death.

"Evergrave Creek," I muttered. "And the bridge is called nothing. There is no name. No listing for any bridge in the area. Hmmm." But I looked at the maps and could see the bridge had to be there. There was no other way to get out of the area, and according to the census, there were homes back that far. "It's got to be there."

I scribbled down a few notes and put everything back the way I found it.

As I left the library, I felt as if I was missing something. As crazy as it seemed, I wanted to go back to County Line Road 63 and take a look around now that the sun was up and I had my wits about me. But that confidence quickly left me when I thought about that eerie silence. I didn't want that kind of quiet. I didn't want to ever be in that kind of quiet again because it wasn't just the lack of sound— it was the way it forced you to listen to yourself.

Had anyone ever really stopped and listened to their own breathing, their heartbeat, the blood pumping in the veins, cells dying and cells rejuvenating, muscles flexing and releasing? It was maddening because all it revealed was that the human person was just a machine that would wind down some day and cease to exist. Those sounds are more natural than the squirrels running around on the forest floor. But we don't hear them because we are too busy living to listen to our bodies slowly dying.

I got in my car and drove to the Brew-Ha-Ha. There, Aunt Astrid was handling the customers, and Kevin Baker was rustling up the grub for the noontime rush.

"Hi." I slipped behind the counter, kissed my aunt on the cheek, and tied a clean white apron around my waist. "Is Bea in yet?"

"She won't be in today. Turns out she found out quite a few things from Jake about that part of town, and the two of them stayed up most of the night talking about it." Aunt Astrid rubbed my back. "But she wants us over to their house tonight for dinner."

"What is she making?" I grunted. "It all depends on what she is making."

"Special for you. Veggie burgers. She told me to tell you. Jake will even cook them on the grill."

"Okay." I reluctantly gave in. A home-cooked meal, even if it was vegan, was better than Spaghettios out of a can.

"Aunt Astrid, you know Bea and Jake didn't stay up all night talking." I raised my right eyebrow and looked at my aunt. "Do you need me to explain to you what married people do?"

Aunt Astrid laughed out loud. So did I. It felt good to be around her and forget about the no-name bridge and Evergrave Creek and that awful silence we heard.

But that night, with my notes from the library in my hand, I wasn't prepared for the next layer of this onion to be peeled away.

Suicide Bridge

❧

"Just keep a sweater on," Bea told me when I walked in her house to find she had the back porch door open. The cold autumn air wafted in. Along with it was the smell of delicious burgers cooking on the grill.

"Oh my gosh." I clapped my gloved hands together. "Do I smell hot dogs, too?"

"How can you tell the difference?" Bea shook her head and looked at me. "It's all on the grill. It all smells the same."

"I told you she'd like it!" Jake yelled in the house from the grill on their deck.

"Bea, grilled veggies, whether they are in vegetable form or molded into patty form, still smell like veggies. But a hot dog is meat. It smells like heaven. I'll bet heaven smells like meat cooking on the grill." Just then, Peanut Butter came rubbing against my leg.

"You agree with me, don't you?" I asked the cat with my mind.

"Yes. But I do wish they'd close the door. Too cold."

"I agree with Cath!" Jake yelled from outside.

"You two are really crazy," Bea replied.

"No, Bea. You and I are crazy," I clarified. "For going out to that county line road last night," I said in a whisper, jerking my thumb in Jake's direction. "What were we thinking?" I wasn't sure what she had told him about our little adventure, but I didn't want to be responsible for the big reveal if she hadn't mentioned it.

"He knows, but he wasn't happy," she replied while handing me a stack of paper plates and napkins to set around the counter.

Bea had a wonderful island in the middle of her massive kitchen, and we all had our assigned seats since we ate there so much.

Within just a few minutes, Jake came in the house with a steaming plate piled high with veggie burgers, Vienna Beef hot dogs, perfectly charred corn on the cob, and baked potatoes wrapped snugly in aluminum foil.

Bea poured everyone a cup of iced tea, and we ate and talked as if it were our last meal.

"So Cath," Jake started, "when my beautiful wife suggests you guys go out ghost hunting in the middle of the night, is it your usual response to say yes?"

I looked at Jake, who was more like a brother to me, and with a mouth full of hot dog, muttered, "Yes."

"Like I told her last night, if you guys have a feeling about something, I'm good with that. But let me know if it takes you anywhere weird, because I might have information that could save you guys a trip. Especially a trip in the middle of the night."

Reasoning with the Wonder Falls chief detective was hard to do. But I loved him for being so accepting of Bea's gifts and of the rest of our quirks.

"It wasn't really in the middle of the night. That would have been crazy. Right, Bea?"

"Yeah, I told you, Jake. It wasn't the middle of the night. We're smarter than that." Bea looked at me and crossed her eyes, making me nearly choke on my second hot dog.

"I put a protection spell on them, Jake. Didn't Bea tell you?" Aunt Astrid chimed in.

"You, too, Astrid?" Jake shook his head and

squinted his eyes. He wiped his mouth and looked at Bea, who gave him a playful wink.

"Well, I don't know about you guys, but I found out some very interesting things about this part of town," I started. I explained how that area had shrunk and expanded every couple of years, how there were always people living out there but not many, and that it was mostly either untamed forest or owned by farmers. Then I mentioned the bridge, and I saw the look on both Bea and Jake's faces.

"We were just out at that bridge." Jake leaned forward as he spoke.

"Who's we?" I asked, looking at Bea.

"Me and Blake," Jake clarified.

I had purposefully avoided not only seeing Blake Samberg but also hearing any mention of him. I knew he was Jake's partner, and I knew he was a good detective, so he wouldn't be leaving Wonder Falls any time soon.

Let's just say we had been through some things together. Things that would bring normal people closer, maybe even attract them to one another. But not with Blake. Instead, after all we went through, he chose to go out with my archenemy from high school, Darla Castellan. The guy faced creeps all day long and chose to date one on his off time, too. I just didn't get it. That was the thanks I got for saving his life. But I didn't say any of this to Jake and nodded for him to continue.

"We call it Suicide Bridge. I don't know what its real name is, if it even has one. But at least once a year we get a call that someone has gone missing. Once all the routine procedures are completed, we'll take a squad car out there and find some poor devil hanging from the girders."

"That's so terrible." Aunt Astrid put her hand to her cheek.

"Yeah." Jake continued, "We just had a call for a missing person about a month ago and had to make the trek out there. Sure enough, the man we were looking for was there."

"Jeez, Jake. That's rough," I said soothingly, adding this to the list of odd facets of Jake's chosen profession. He knew the Greenstone women fought monsters, but he didn't seem to realize how similar he and Bea really were. The only difference was that *his* monsters were bound by the laws of physics. "My gosh. I'm sorry you've got to see those things."

"It was Archie Jones," Bea added.

"Archie Jones?" Aunt Astrid gasped again. "You mean that sweet little man who sells his skin-care products at the farmers' market?"

Bea nodded.

"Oh my God!" I blurted out. "He was the guy with the basil-and-lime body lotion and soap, wasn't he? Man, I loved that stuff. It smelled so good. Well, good luck ever finding that combination of scents anywhere else on the planet."

"Bea." Jake furrowed his brow. "I thought we weren't going to mention who it was until all the details had been sorted out."

"I'm sorry." Bea put her hand on her husband's strong arm. "Whether you like it or not, finding that man has an effect on you, too. That's where I come in. Secrets don't help."

"She's right, honey," Aunt Astrid stated. She looked Jake right in the eye.

It was interesting to watch the dynamics among everyone here. Jake loved Bea with all his heart, and that was obvious. He and I joked as though we'd been raised in matching cribs. But when it came to Aunt Astrid, there was a mutual respect there. They were both professionals and excelled at their chosen crafts. In Aunt Astrid's case, it just happened to be witchcraft.

"I don't need to know about that case," she said. "Go ahead and keep the files closed on that. But when you are the one who comes across a scene where a lost soul has taken their own life, you need to have the residue of that scene wiped away."

"I understand that, Astrid." Jake patted her hand. "The reason why I didn't want to discuss the details is because we aren't sure this is a suicide."

Now that was better. Not that it was better that poor Archie Jones was murdered. From a mystical point of view, the collateral damage was practically nil. It might sound morbid, but it was true. Suicide made everyone question themselves. Murder, well, that made everyone question their neighbor. It wasn't perfect. It was just how it was.

"Well, you didn't say that," Bea protested.

"Bea, I'm a detective. I'm not the *Wonder Falls Inquirer*." He gave her a quizzical look. "Handing out details surrounding a body that we found isn't my job. So, now, you guys already know too much."

"Don't worry, Jake," I announced. "Your secrets are safe with me. I can't speak for these other two."

I reached for another hot dog from the platter. Without being noticed, I broke off a small piece and dropped it on the floor to be gobbled up by my furry friend.

Archibald K. Jones

❧❀❧

Archie Jones's death was listed in the Wonder Falls obituaries three days later. There was not going to be any wake or funeral.

"The body still has to be looked over. It's considered evidence until they can figure out a few more things." Bea washed her hands in the sink at the café.

"Have you heard any more about what happened?" Aunt Astrid looked at Bea with concern.

"Only what I overheard Jake and Blake talking about yesterday when I brought them lunch at the station. It's peculiar to say the least."

"Peculiar. That's right up our alley." I wiped down a recently vacated table and then made my way to the counter. We had a quiet morning, with just a few folks taking up space, all with their heads buried in some kind of electronic device. I never understood the attraction. But it made for happy and frequent customers. I leaned in toward Bea and folded my arms in front of me.

"Archie was hanging off the bridge. There was a makeshift noose around his neck made of pieces of clothing like a jacket, shoelaces, and then a scarf. So if he was planning on killing himself, he decided to do it at the last minute. But there were other things, too."

"What other things?" I asked.

"He had traces of ketamine in his system." Bea wiped the counter more out of habit than because it was dirty.

"What is ketamine?" Aunt Astrid leaned in closer so we wouldn't be overheard by the patrons.

"It's a horse tranquilizer." Bea wrinkled her nose. "Apparently it is also used by people who want to... get high on horse tranquilizers." She shook her head and shrugged.

"That doesn't make any sense," I said. "Archie was, well, like Bea. Out there huggin' trees and going all holistic. I mean, his business was all-natural beauty products. He might have been a bit goofy, but that doesn't jibe with a guy who'd swallow a horse pill. It's not like that would be an easy task. Have you ever seen the size of those things?"

"He wouldn't have swallowed a whole pill." Aunt Astrid's voice was low. "He would have ground it up and snorted it or injected it with something else. But you're right, Cath. It doesn't sound like Archie Jones."

"I also heard Blake say there were marks around his wrists. Like he may have been tied up before he died."

My aunt just shook her head.

I stepped away from the counter, grabbing the coffee pot as I did, and made a quick lap around the dining area, refilling cups and clearing away plates. But as I stepped back up to the counter, I had a burning question.

"Does anyone know where Archie lived?" The map images from the library were tickling at my brain, and I wasn't sure why but felt there was something to it. In fact, I was already pretty sure I knew what Bea was going to say before she said it.

"He had a small farm in Wonder Falls proper." She put her hand on her hip and looked at me. "But that's too far from County Line Road 63, isn't it?"

"I'm not sure." I put my hands up as if I were surrendering. "I think I might need to go back to the library and check. Plus, in the census information the librarian showed me, we can find out the names and history of the families that have lived there."

"That's a good idea. I'll join you." Aunt Astrid reached for her jacket that was hanging on a peg behind the counter. "Bea, can you handle the café until we get back?"

"Sure, Mom." Bea smiled.

"What are you thinking?" I asked my aunt as she climbed into the passenger seat of my car.

"I'm not sure either, honey. I'm hoping something will come to me when I see it."

The same librarian with the ring in her nose was working the information desk when my aunt and I walked in. I pointed in the direction of the Wonder Falls archive room, and she smiled broadly, giving me a nod of approval.

"My gosh. All the years I've been coming to this library, and I don't think I've ever been in this little room."

"Right?" I quickly reached for the maps. "I thought that exact same thing when I was here the other day. Okay. Here's the latest map from three years ago. I'd venture to say not much has changed from then until now, wouldn't you?"

"I'm more interested in the maps of the past couple decades."

By the time Aunt Astrid was satisfied she was looking at the right maps, we had almost completely covered the conference table that was in this room.

I watched her as she studied them. Moving her hands back and forth as if she was trying to find something, she walked back and forth from one map to the next.

Finally, she took the latest map and slid it over a map from over seventy-five years ago.

"Look here." She pointed to an area of farmland. "It was only in the last three years that this tiny little bit of land was separated from this bigger part. The town must have reassigned the boundaries."

"So what does that mean?"

"The owner of this massive area of farmland probably didn't like that. It can cause all kinds of problems with taxes, farming regulations—heck, even water, trash collection, sewers." She squinted as she studied the lines. "And it looks like this small piece of land had been part of the bigger estate since Wonder Falls started charting the town maps this way."

"I'm still not following." I scratched my head. "Road 63 is way over here. The bridge they found Archie Jones at is also way over here." I waved my hand over two areas of the map that my aunt wasn't looking at. "What does that little piece of land have to do with Archie Jones?"

"That little piece of land is where his farm was."

I blinked with surprise.

"How do you know that?"

She looked at me and winked. "How can we find the purchase agreements of these properties?"

"The librarian said they were all in the library database. But she said if we were looking for something specific, it would help to have names and dates and stuff."

"Boot her up, and let's see what we can find."

I wasn't sure what kind of rabbit hole my aunt was leading me down. But I quickly put the maps back, grabbed two chairs, and hunkered down in front of the computer to search for whatever she told me. It was a matter of minutes before she clapped and pointed at the screen.

"That's it!" she cried excitedly before blushing and pounding her forehead with the palm of her hand. "Sorry. I forgot we were in the library," she whispered.

She pointed to the words Short Form Individual Deed of Trust. The name on it was one Archibald K. Jones.

"You were right," I mumbled. "How did you know?"

"Some things I don't ask how but rather just say thank you to the forces guiding us."

As I skimmed the document, glossing over the legal mumbo jumbo, I saw the description of the land. It was just a small plot of 4.2 acres. Hardly what I'd call a farm compared to the property that surrounded it on the map.

"Look. There are other documents with Archie's name on them." The database had an ongoing listing of legal documents ranging from the validity of the property lines of Archie's land to the timeliness of closing on the deed to unauthorized dumping on the land. It was a sea of legal red tape attached to that small sliver of land.

"I hate to say it, but if I was going through all this legal garbage, I might hang myself, too." I know it was crass, but let's face it. Nothing sucks out the will to fight more than the prospect of going to court or being sued. At least astral spiders can be destroyed in the privacy of your own home without lawyers being present or fees accruing.

"You aren't just whistling Dixie," my aunt replied. "But all of these things have been filed by different people. Either Archie Jones had a lot of enemies, or there was a conspiracy against him. Look."

It was true. There wasn't just one person's name on the filed documents. There was Mr. Reginald Tinder, who was suing for the unauthorized dumping. Mr. Linus Hoage filed against Archie for missing the deadline to close on the deed. And there were half a dozen other names of men accusing Archie of breaking some kind of law or procedure.

"But what do they all mean? What were they trying to get? Money?" I looked to my aunt.

"That's all I can think of. Maybe Archie Jones was a wealthier man than we all knew."

"So who owns his land now that he's dead? He wasn't married."

"I don't know." My aunt gave me a sideways glance. "Maybe we should take a drive out there and see. Maybe one of us would like to buy a farm."

"Aunt Astrid, the last time we pretended to be interested in buying property, it was the Prestwick house, and that didn't turn out all that well, did it?"

My heart twinged at the thought of that house. It

was where Blake Samberg realized I was just too weird for him.

"Point taken." She put her hand in mine. She knew that experience had left the deepest wound on me, and it hadn't completely healed yet. She smoothed my ponytail and then scooted her chair out. "Then let's just go snooping and see what we see."

Lunatic Farmers

❧❧❧

Getting to the late Archie Jones's farmhouse was an adventure in itself. There were half a dozen gravel roads that snuck through cornfields and patches of forest running along the back side of Wonder Falls proper. Driving down these roads made me feel as though we were sneaking up on the place. The good part was no one saw us. The bad part was no one saw us.

"I have no idea where I'm at." I stared out the windshield, positive I had seen that exact same row of corn ten minutes ago.

"Don't worry. I can see where we are." My aunt certainly saw different landmarks and scenery than I did. From the look on her face, I could tell she wasn't all that keen on the neighborhood. "But when I say it's time to go, no questions."

I let out a deep breath and hit the gas. The grumble of the gravel underneath my car was loud and made the same sound in my ears as when I ate my favorite cereal, Cap'n Crunch.

Finally, a tiny house of red brick and white stucco appeared off a long gravel driveway up a hill. Wild and unruly bushes and shrubs flanked the house on all sides. The trees also hung dangerously low to the roof, which had broken twigs collecting on it. A few sprouts were peeking from the gutters, which obviously hadn't been cleaned for a while.

"What the heck?" I stopped the car and looked at the sad state of the house. "It looks like no one has lived here for at least a year."

When the engine cut off, I opened the door and listened. Birds. An airplane overhead. Sounds. I got out and looked at my aunt, who stared at the house intently.

She took her steps as she always did, slowly and with careful deliberation. Some people might think she was handicapped or in some kind of pain and that was what made her move so slowly. The truth was that she had to maneuver between several dimensions at once.

"This is a mess," she said. "This whole place is just a mess." She pointed to the roof and the ground, but I knew she was seeing more than me.

"I'm going to look inside." I walked up to the windows, which were all free of curtains or blinds of any kind. Inside, the entire place was empty. There wasn't a single piece of furniture or picture on the wall, and as I looked in the kitchen window around the side of the house, I saw that there wasn't even a bar of soap left behind. Usually, there was something to indicate someone had been there recently. But not here.

"It is empty. Like a Dunkin Donuts box in a kindergarten classroom." I pointed to the window. "And it looks like it's been empty for longer than three days. Do you think Archie moved out and then killed himself?"

"Hey!" came a very angry voice from behind us. We spun around to see a man in dirty brown pants and a gray-and-blue flannel shirt come stomping toward us. "What are you doing up here?"

"I'm sorry." My aunt spoke up, squinting at the man while waving a friendly hello. "My name is Astrid Greenstone, and this is my niece, Cath. We were friends of the late Archie…"

"I don't care who you are," he growled. "This here is private property."

"We were friends of Archie Jones and wondering…." My explanation was cut short as a huge black pickup with massive black wheels skidded to a halt behind my car. It looked as if it had made it through a landmine and made my beater look like a Hot Wheels version next to a Tonka Truck. The driver hopped out of the car, leaving the engine rumbling, and stomped up to stand next to the guy yelling at us.

"Did you know Archie?" I asked innocently, looking between the two men.

"I'm going to tell you this one thing, girlie-girl. You get back in your car, and you two get off my property." He pulled his shirt aside to reveal the biggest hunting knife I had ever seen in my life. I swallowed hard, took my aunt by her hand, and quickly led her to my car. We climbed in, and before I even shut my door, the engine was running and the car was in drive.

With the gravel driveway being wide enough for my little car, I turned around and carefully drove off the property, respectful not to kick up the gravel at the men standing there. I had to go into the grass a little to avoid hitting the truck, not that any damage would have been noticed among the dirt and dents already there.

"What in the world was that about?" I gasped as we pulled back onto the gravel road that got us there. Before I could relax, I looked in the rearview mirror to see the giant truck quickly following behind us. "Looks like we're getting an escort."

"This is bad." My aunt grasped the door handle with one hand and braced her other hand on the dashboard. "Can you go any faster?"

"I could probably get up to eighty miles an hour, but I think I'd lose control and dump us over into the ditch if I tried."

The truck revved its engine and lurched dangerously close to my rear bumper. He honked his horn, an obnoxiously loud barking sound that reverberated in my chest. I could see him laughing inside the cab and bouncing in his seat as if this were the most fun.

Part of me wanted to slam on the brakes and let him plow into my car. I'd see how long that smile stayed on his face. But with Aunt Astrid sitting next to me, it was impossible. Plus the fact that that truck, with its steel grille and giant tires, would probably plow right over me, crushing my only mode of transportation, with me inside. If the guy was willing to threaten a woman with a weapon, he would have no problem with a hit and run.

"What is wrong with this guy?" I whined. "How far does he plan on chasing us?"

As if he heard what I said, the guy slammed on the monster truck's brakes, and it quickly became smaller and smaller in the rearview mirror. I felt my shoulders relax, then my breathing came out in deep gasps, and my hands loosened on the steering wheel. Stretching them, I heard them crack as I flexed my poor fingers.

"Aunt Astrid?"

"Yes, dear?" My aunt's tone was almost funny.

"What did you see while we were there?" I waited as my aunt looked into her hands for a moment. Her jaw moved as if she was about to say something but then thought maybe not, but reconsidered again. I looked at the road, which had finally become asphalt, and relaxed even more at the sight of another car passing us in the opposite direction.

"Aunt Astrid?" I patted her leg. "Are you all right?"

"This is worse than I thought." She chuckled nervously. "I wasn't prepared for what I saw. Nor was I prepared for those two gentlemen back there."

"Who could have seen that coming?" I almost

laughed. "Lunatic hillbillies are only in movies. Honestly, I don't even know if you'd call them hillbillies. Lunatic farmers? Overseers? What were they doing at Archie's place? They said it was private property. Do you think Archie was related to those guys? Maybe they were the ones who emptied out his house."

"That house was empty for a lot longer than three days." My aunt kneaded her hands. "What was I thinking suggesting we come up here?"

"Aunt Astrid, it's okay. No harm. No foul." I tried to soothe her, but something else was the matter, and she wasn't ready to tell me what it was. "Do you want to go back to the café? Maybe you need Bea."

"No." She spat the word quickly. "Cath, please take me home."

I nodded and didn't push. But I don't need to explain that this had me not just worried about my aunt but also angry that two men put her in such a state. If she wasn't ready to talk to Bea, I was.

Speak of the Devil

❧❀❧

"Jake is going to stop by in a little while." Bea tossed a chickpea-and-spinach salad with tiny chopped tomatoes, shavings of aged Parmesan cheese, and rye croutons. It was a hit with the café patrons. Even I thought it was a nice bowl to try.

But I could tell by her voice she was angry.

"What for?" I asked.

"To tell us if those men who chased you had any prior convictions or records. If they are violent people, if criminal behavior is in their past, you can bet we won't be going back up that way without our own protection."

I looked at my aunt, who looked much better than she had yesterday after our ordeal with the mad farmers. But even though the color was back in her cheeks and her eyes twinkled like usual, she wasn't saying much. She still hadn't told Bea or me what she had seen at the house. I guessed she was just waiting for the right moment. Maybe she was even waiting for some kind of sign or a tip from one of her alternate dimensions.

"Speak of the devil." Aunt Astrid pointed to the door. Setting off the tinkling wind-chime bells at the door were Jake and his partner, Blake. I wasn't expecting both of them and had hoped Jake would come alone. Thankfully, a familiar fuzziness rubbed up against my leg. I looked down to see Treacle had slunk in through the back door by the kitchen and come to see me.

"*What brings you around?*" I extended my arms to him, and he jumped up into them.

"*It's quiet in town. Nothing much is going on.*" He bumped his head affectionately on my chin then squirmed out of my arms and onto the table I was standing next to. I let him go but was thankful he stayed close enough for me to divert my eyes from Blake if necessary.

Of course, Blake showed up in his no-nonsense suit and shined shoes, looking all dapper and handsome. Wasn't it just like him to do something so mean.

"Hey, Bea." Jake leaned over the counter, giving his wife an affectionate kiss before greeting the rest of us. "Greenstones." He smiled broadly.

"Hello, Jake. Detective Samberg, you're looking well." Aunt Astrid folded her arms over her chest.

"Thank you, Astrid. You, too." He looked over at me, but suddenly, Treacle had become the object of my undivided interest. I didn't dare look at him for fear I might just burst into tears right there.

"So." Bea saved the day by piping up immediately. "Did you find out anything?"

"Those fellows you described are Otto and Leland Clare. They are a couple of odd birds. Father and son. But we've got no files on them. By all accounts, they are just territorial." Jake looked at Aunt Astrid and me with his eyebrows raised. "Probably just didn't like people on his property."

"We weren't on his property." Aunt Astrid spoke firmly. "We went to see Archie Jones's place. He owned those couple of acres, didn't he?"

"He did for a short while." Blake spoke while withdrawing his annoying little notebook out of his inside jacket pocket. "But the Clares bought it after Archie died."

"Sounds like they were studying the obituaries, waiting for that to happen," I blurted out, looking at Bea and Jake. "Isn't that a little weird?"

"Weird, maybe. But not against the law," Blake stated in that annoying know-it-all tone he used with me.

The words *why don't you shut up* surfaced in my mouth. They tasted like sweet strawberries, so help me they did. But I didn't say them. Instead, I looked at Aunt Astrid, who looked at me knowingly. I was not sure if it was because we encountered something different at that property than what Jake and Blake were reporting to us or because she knew I wanted to tell Blake where the door was.

As she was about to speak, the door opened up, and everything in the Brew-Ha-Ha changed.

"Hello, ladies!" came the deep and soothing voice of Tom Warner. He was in his uniform, looking handsome and confident. My cheeks went up in flames, and I couldn't stop my lips from smiling.

"Officer Warner." Bea also smiled and waved. "Where have you been hiding?"

"Believe me," he cooed, knowing he was such a hit with all the Greenstone women, "I'd have been around a lot more if Cath would let me." He looked at me with those incredible eyes and winked. I shook my head.

"What are you talking about?" I said. "You can come by any time you like. It's a free country."

He came sauntering up to me, making quite a spectacle, and struck a typical policeman pose, with his hands resting on his utility belt and his weight on his right foot.

"You were right, Aunt Astrid." He looked to her. "I guess all I had to do was ask."

I glared at my aunt, who giggled, doing nothing but encouraging Tom to be even bolder.

The truth was, I really liked Tom. We had met at the Muskox Serenity Spa and Retreat Center when there was a mysterious murder and astral spiders. He was making a scene today just to be funny, but he had a quiet confidence about him. Most importantly, he was very open minded.

Of course, I didn't tell him everything about my background, the paranormal experiences that one if not all of us Greenstones have on a daily basis, or the truly scary things that have happened to us, to *me*. But he wasn't afraid of the things I'd shared with him so far. My family liked him. That was important, too.

"Quit flirting with my aunt." I folded my arms

over my chest. Without hesitating, Tom came up and began to pet Treacle on the head. Both toms seemed to have developed a mutual affection for each other, but I couldn't say when that happened.

"You, too, Treacle?" I shook my head at the feline, who purred loudly.

"He's a good one, Cath. I can't help myself." The purring was so loud it vibrated the table.

"What brings you to this part of town?" I rocked back and forth on my heels.

"I was hoping you might be free tonight. We could take in a movie and get something to eat." He had no shame. The guy was not afraid to say what he wanted in front of everyone. I wasn't used to this kind of brazen behavior, but I did like how it left no room for interpretation.

"Yeah. That sounds nice." I let out my breath. "Hey, question for you. Have you ever had any dealings with a couple of guys... What are their names again?" I looked at Jake, but Blake answered.

"Otto and Leland Clare," Blake muttered. "But as we said, we have no..."

"The Clares? Good grief. What have they done now?"

I looked at Tom, wide eyed.

"You've heard of these guys?" I put my hand on

Tom's strong bicep and felt him flex underneath his shirt. What a ham. How I enjoyed him.

"Not as much as we used to." Tom turned to face everyone in the café. "You boys probably don't have much on them. I think only about three acres of their one hundred and forty acres fall on Wonder Falls proper. We've got a file on them over three inches thick."

Jake's eyes widened. Blake put away his notebook and looked intently at Tom.

"What have they done?" Bea put her hand to her throat.

"Well, I couldn't say exactly without looking in the file. But I know for the years I've been on the force we've been out to their farm many times because one of their neighbors has called us out there. The calls are for one of two things. Either the elder Otto Clare is trespassing on the neighboring farms, or they've been starving their livestock."

"What?" I gasped.

Tom nodded, his eyebrows coming together.

"It's terrible," he said. Looking around the café, he lowered his voice so as not to disturb the patrons that were busy eating, drinking, and texting. He took me by the hand and pulled me along with him closer to my aunt. "We've removed horses, dogs, cats—all of them in various stages of starvation—on at least three occasions. They try and chew their way out of the barn he locks them in. The dogs and cats are in cages in the house. Most of them have to be put down once a rescue team arrives."

"Why does he do this?" I asked, looking at Treacle. I couldn't imagine something like that happening to my cat. What kind of person does that?

"He has no answer when he's hauled into court." I could see Tom's jaw working as if he was trying to keep his emotions in check. "He just pays the fine and sits in the jailhouse for thirty days, maybe sixty days."

"My gosh." Aunt Astrid looked angry, too. "Is he doing that now?"

"I couldn't say." Tom shrugged. "We haven't had any calls to the farm. But the greedy guy has also bought up the property around him. It's not like anyone can just go and take a drive or a walk up there. The farm is right smack in the middle of a couple dozen acres. I wouldn't want to be caught snooping around on the Clare farm without a small army."

I looked at my aunt. We both realized we may have really just escaped a much more serious situation than we thought.

"That is really horrible." Bea rubbed her stomach. Jake, seeing her distress, instinctively reached for her hand. They looked at each other with an understanding that I'd like to think most married people developed over their years together. It was a strength that spread to the rest of us and even gave me hope that there were men out there who could accept the challenge of being married to a witch. My eyes flicked over to Blake, who was staring at Tom then at me. I let my eyes linger for a split second and then turned to Tom.

"What happens when you get a call to go out there? Do you go by yourself or…"

Tom started to laugh.

"I might be brave, but I'm not that brave. Like I said. I wouldn't go out there without a small army. There are usually two units that will go there, and they've got shotguns in addition to their pistols."

The breath caught in my throat.

"But…" Tom shook his head. "Truthfully, we've never had to use them. Never once has any shot ever been fired on the Clare property by one of our officers. It's just that the area is so remote, and well, they are a bit crazy out there."

My mind began to whirl, and I was feeling an overwhelming desire to do something stupid. I kept my mouth shut and waited. No matter what anyone said, I was going to snoop around on that property. If there were animals in trouble, I was going to help.

"That might be some information the Wonder Falls PD should have." Jake looked at Tom and nodded.

"Absolutely," Tom agreed. "I'll get the complete file on these guys over to you. Can I send it to your attention?"

"That'll work." Jake reached out his hand to Tom, and they shook.

"If you don't mind my asking, what are you looking into them for? Have they done something?" Tom looked at me.

How was I going to explain this?

"I'll tell you all about it over dinner," I quickly jumped in.

I certainly didn't want to get into all the gory details in front of Blake and listen to a lecture on trespassing. Even though neither Aunt Astrid nor I knew we were trespassing. We were just exploring. There weren't any signs. But even I knew that was a pretty flimsy defense. I don't have a Do Not Trespass sign on my house, but I think most people know not to walk right in and start taking a bath in my tub.

"I can't wait." Tom's eyes twinkled like a boy who

was given a reward for returning a lost wallet. "It was nice to see all of you again." He turned and gave Bea a wave. He shook Aunt Astrid's hand in both of his own.

"Tom, You should come by for dinner sometime. That one is constantly mooching off of us for a home-cooked meal." Jake jerked his thumb at me and, like a true brother, embarrassed me at every chance. "You are more than welcome to come along." I rolled my eyes at him.

"I think I'll just do that," Tom replied.

"Why don't you leave your schedule open for Friday night, Tom?" Bea jumped in, smiling devilishly at me.

"Yes. Friday night is lentil loaf night. You don't want to miss that," I shot back.

"How did you know I love lentils? Practically raised on them. Fridays, we didn't eat meat in my house, so this will really remind me of my childhood."

"I can't win," I mumbled. "See you tonight?"

"About seven?"

"Yeah. Meet me here."

"It's a date."

Tom gave another quick wave and then dashed out the door. I let out a deep breath and walked over to Treacle, who had stretched out on the table next to the window, soaking up the sun that was beating down on him. His fur was warm to the touch, and he began to purr.

"*I really like him.*" He looked at me with eyes that were barely slits.

"*I do, too.*"

"Well, that's a lot of news for one day," Jake said. "We better get back to work."

"I'd like to get ahold of that file on the Clares, too," Blake mumbled. "That's a little too close to home for my taste."

"You've got that right," Jake concurred.

Before they left, Bea wrapped up a couple of turkey sandwiches with two containers of the salad she was mixing just as they walked in and, much to my dismay, shaved off two healthy slices of peach pie that I was planning on eating.

"Okay. I'm going to say it. That Tom Warner is smitten with you." Aunt Astrid giggled like a hyena.

"My gosh! Isn't he?" Bea chimed in. "It's so cute! Especially how you get all shy and blushy around him."

"I do not." I grimaced.

Both Bea and my aunt started to laugh so loud the patrons who had up until now been in their own worlds looked up to see what all the hubbub was about.

"*Yes, you do,*" Treacle added as the tip of his tail waved at me lazily.

"Ugh. You guys are all impossible," I scoffed, secretly loving it. "So what do you think of what he said about the Clares?"

It was as if I'd thrown a bucket of ice water at both of them. They were no longer smiling.

"I think we were lucky to get out of there." Aunt Astrid pushed herself up from the small table she always sat at. "I could tell by the look on your face, you were thinking of going up there." She didn't look at me as she spoke. I was about to protest when Bea spoke up.

"I just thought that if there was that kind of suffering going on, I might be able to help," Bea protested. "Those men just get a fine and a few weeks in jail for torture?"

I bit my tongue. Apparently, Aunt Astrid picked up on Bea thinking of a visit to the Clare Farm and not me. Well, I wasn't going alone. I was bringing a police officer with me, hopefully, if he agreed to trespassing and spying as part of our date tonight.

"Don't go up there, Bea." Aunt Astrid's voice was

stern when she turned and looked at me. "The place isn't safe, right, Cath?"

"Well, from what we've seen and heard so far, I'd guess no. It isn't safe." I thought back to Tamara's encounter the other day. "So why would a farmer starve his animals? And what, if anything, does that have to do with the thing that was scratching at Tamara's car, and the soul parasite?"

"I'm not sure." Aunt Astrid put a hand on her hip. "But Bea is right about one thing. If we are going to solve this mystery, it is going to require we go to that farm and survey the land. We just need to prepare."

In my mind, that kind of preparation required recon. Someone had to get the lay of the land in case we needed to make a quick getaway or hide somewhere. I'd already decided it would be me. With or without Tom, I was going to do some snooping.

"Well, I guess I've got a date tonight," I mused. "I'm going to be busy. You two will have to scheme without me and fill me in on the details tomorrow."

"Of course. What are you going to wear?" Bea asked. "If there is anything of mine you'd like to borrow, just say so."

"Would you like me to cast an olfactory spell on you? It'll make you smell like vanilla all night. Men find that a soothing scent that prompts them to be more honest than if they were smelling, say, jungle gardenia or hemp." Aunt Astrid said this as if she were asking me if I had my keys, wallet, and four gallons of water before heading out for a journey into the desert.

"No," I said.

"How about a quick aura cleanse? It makes your cheeks naturally rosy," Bea offered, batting her eyelashes.

I was about to speak when a new customer came into the café.

"Hi. Welcome to the Brew-Ha-Ha. These women are crazy." I smiled, my eyebrows up in my forehead as I pointed to my aunt and cousin.

Paranormal Catastrophe

"I didn't think you'd be up for this at all," I said, smiling at Tom over my chocolate milkshake. I had just finished a cheeseburger with everything and Cajun fries, and he had devoured a pork chop the size of a starter log, when I suggested we go on an epic journey to drop a ring into the fires on Mount Doom. Okay, so it wasn't that epic. But after what happened with Aunt Astrid and the stories about the animals Tom had told us, I was sure there was a need to go onto the Clare property.

"Well, it probably isn't the smartest move for a police officer to make. I doubt we'll find anything, but let's just say I've got a gut feeling, and that counts for something on the police force." He winked at me, making me smile.

"Yeah," I concurred. "I've got sort of a sixth sense, too."

"You probably mean that more literally, don't you?"

I stared at Tom for a minute while he wiped his mouth with his napkin. Should I tell him a little more about my gift? About Aunt Astrid and Bea? No. I wouldn't say anything about them. Their gifts weren't mine to share. I'd just stick to my own abilities. Maybe. I didn't know.

"I guess I do."

He leaned closer to me, and I could smell his cologne. It was a wonderfully clean smell, like freesia or something.

"Can you see the future?"

No, but my aunt Astrid can. I thought of blurting that out but changed my mind and just shook my head no.

"Well, I trust your sixth sense. If what you told me about your experience with your aunt is true, then it is suspicious behavior if nothing else."

Talking to Tom was such a refreshing change from "Mr. Do Everything By The Book" that I felt as if I wanted to kiss him. Instead, I smiled and nodded while not a single word of response popped into my head.

Finally, I snapped out of it.

"Then we better get going."

Tom drove us in his bright-red pickup truck to a remote area where County Line Road 63 intersected with 314 West. He backed the truck into a small alcove that was almost completely concealed by wild-growing trees and shrubs. Surprisingly, the truck had all but disappeared from view.

"Speed trap." Tom looked at me and winked.

"You get a lot of traffic down these roads?"

"Not 63. But 314 West goes straight to the next town of Lemont. A lot of kids go down this road and think no one is around."

"Oh, the ignorance of youth." I sighed. "Remember being that careless?"

"You mean as opposed to the monument of maturity that I am now as I sneak onto some weird farmer's property?" He crossed his eyes at me, making me laugh.

We climbed out of the truck, and I listened.

"Come on." Tom took my hand. "I think the farm is north of here."

I squeezed it tightly as we walked through the brush.

"So why do you think a person would starve their

animals? I mean, that sounds like a symptom of mental illness. Why would he just be fined or put in jail? Should he be given a psych evaluation or something?" My voice was just loud enough to be heard over the dry, crunching leaves and twigs.

"The police can recommend it. The courts can, too." Tom stretched his leg to get over a small ditch then turned and offered me his other hand to help me across. "But it is up to that person or their family to make it happen. If they don't think they need it, then they won't get it. There isn't anything we can do about it."

"That's sad." For a second, I felt pity for the Clare family. I couldn't believe that anyone would intentionally torture an animal and be cruel just because they could. But then a scary thought entered my mind. "Is it true that people who hurt animals are just priming the pump before they move on to…people?"

"That's a theory that seems to have some legs," Tom said. "It is usually the case."

We walked in silence for a while, covering a big chunk of territory. I was glad he was holding my hand, and as the sun started to set, I realized my eyes were starting to play tricks on me. The shadows appeared to be creeping toward our feet, and the branches of the trees seemed to be lowering their canopy closer to our heads. Tom didn't seem to notice, so I kept my mouth shut. I could still hear the sounds of nature, so I kept my cool. That was, until I saw the stagnant water in the gully and the broken-up bridge above it.

"Whoa," Tom whispered. "I've never seen this before. Didn't even know it was here."

"This must be where Archie Jones committed suicide."

"What?" Tom turned to me, his eyes wide.

"Archie Jones. The guy whose farm my aunt and I went to. They found him hanging here and said it looked like suicide. But there were a couple of odd things about it that Jake hasn't elaborated on yet. Foul play might be more like it."

"This is a really lonely place to end your life." Tom crossed himself, and I thought he said a quick prayer. But my gut told me this was a place where prayers got choked up in the tree branches and never made it to the ears of anyone who could help.

The bridge looked like a concrete tongue stretching to reach the other side of the embankment. The guardrails along the sides had long been broken off, leaving pointy, rusty metal spokes protruding from the concrete like rotten teeth.

Someone from the township had visited the bridge at some time. A plastic orange barricade that I'd seen at construction sites was strung along where the guardrails used to be, not that they could save anyone who was falling off the side. It was drooping and sagging in several places.

Other people had visited the bridge as well. Faded graffiti of crude pentagrams, obscene words, and gang symbols had been spray-painted underneath the bridge on the concrete walls that managed to remain standing.

The gully had a good bit of water in it still from the severe thunderstorm when Tamara had her scare. But as we inched our way closer, I noticed something strange about the ground. In the fading sunlight, it looked to me as if the grass and small plants were dead. Not just hibernating with the coming of winter but actually dead. As though salt had been scattered along this place.

"You picking up on anything?" Tom asked me. His voice was serious and full of concern.

"Just the plant life seems to have given up around here. And whoever painted those things under the bridge ought to go back to art class to learn a thing or two."

I let go of Tom's hand and went closer to the bridge. From where I was standing, I could see holes up through it. Even riding a bike across this would have been dangerous. It had appeared from a distance that the bridge had crumbled just feet from the other side, but actually, the same rusted spokes jutted out from the concrete and plunged deep into the earth on the other side. They were like sickly exposed tendons desperately clinging to solid bone.

Bea would have been the person to bring here. She would have been able to pick up on something, I was sure of it. As for me, I just had a serious case of the willies.

"So Mr. Jones would have to have tied his rope to one of those pillars and jumped." Tom pointed to the top side of the bridge. "I don't get it."

"What?" I asked.

"Why here?" He looked around. "Why would anyone come all this way out here and…"

"*Where are you?*"

It was like a child's voice.

"*Where are you? Where are you? I'll find you.*" It became gravelly and angry. "*I'll find you!*"

"What is that?" Tom's expression changed, and I

could see his police training kick in as if a switch had been thrown. I shrugged. Afraid to move my feet for fear of making noise, I swiveled my head and torso around to look behind me. When I faced Tom again, I saw it behind him.

"There's something coming back there." I pointed over his shoulder. It seemed to weave in and out of shadows, but whatever it was, its white night-clothes gave away its position. It was getting closer.

I grabbed Tom by the hand and dashed toward the wall of dirt that the rusty spokes were still connected to. A tree had fallen next to it, offering not just cover but also a piece of nature in the process of decay. It was giving its last bit of essence to the world around it. In its degeneration, it gave life to so many other creatures. I tapped into that power and, whispering a simple spell I used to use during games of hide-and-seek with Bea, held on tightly to Tom's hand as we spied the thing that was approaching.

"*Where are you?*" It kept calling in this singsong way that would transform into a hateful hiss. "*I'll find you! I'll find you!*"

It hobbled the way Tamara had described the thing she had seen. Its body twisted and jerked as it walked, tilting its head around in unnatural positions as it did so. But whatever it was, it wasn't crippled. It moved with surprising skill across the uneven landscape as if it had done this a thousand times before. That had to be what allowed it to run.

It ran in horrific quick steps up to a large oak tree. The trunk of it had to be three feet across. I could have sworn I heard it groan as the creature ran up to it. Stopping unnaturally fast, it stood there like a child that had been given a time out in a corner, and both Tom and I could hear it mumbling. The words weren't audible, but it spat them out. Whatever it was saying, I would bet it wasn't very nice. It jerked and convulsed as it argued at the base of this tree, and Tom and I could only sit there, frozen, and watch in terrified fascination.

"What is it?" Tom whispered.

I squeezed his hand.

The thing whirled around and pointed a contorted claw in our direction.

"*Where are you?*" it hissed again.

Instinctively, Tom shielded me with his body, pushing us down even farther behind the fallen tree. I was sure my little spell was working, but I had no idea if this creature could see past it. Both of us were holding our breath, listening as the thing kept asking where we were.

Then everything shifted. I listened and couldn't hear anything anymore. No birds. No wind, nothing but my own heartbeat. Before I could move a muscle, I looked at Tom. He raised his eyebrows and without a word looked toward his hip. I followed his gaze and saw the holster and gun strapped to him beneath his coat.

I didn't move, but I blinked at him. There was no way to tell him that his gun wouldn't do him any good in this particular situation.

Then I heard it. As if someone had let a bloodhound run loose in the woods and it was on the other side of the log we were hiding behind, something was trying to sniff us out. As it had done on Tamara's car window, it began to scratch and dig at the log and the air in frustration.

I was afraid my spell was going to crack under the psychic pressure of this horror, but just as I was racing through my mind, trying to find something that could teleport us to Cancun, the thing screamed. It was inside and outside of us.

Tom's face said it all. The color dropped from his cheeks, and he blinked in confusion. When he looked at me, the screaming stopped.

We lay still for a while. I didn't dare peek over the tree trunk for fear that creature would be staring at me with blind, white eyes that didn't see my body but seared into my soul.

Tom was the first one to look.

"Did you see that?" he mumbled. "You did, right? You heard that thing. You saw it. I wasn't hallucinating."

"Nope." I choked. "I saw it too."

Tom got to his knees and stood up, extending his hand to me to help me up. His posture was straight. He looked around and had yet to let go of my hand.

"Do you have any idea what that was? Because I've never seen anything like that in my life. Nope. Nothing like that ever. And I'm a cop. I've seen it all. At least I thought I had up until two minutes ago."

I chuckled nervously.

"No. But I think I know someone who would know."

"Let me guess. Your aunt Astrid?"

I wasn't sure if I should be happy he knew the correct answer or not. We had just escaped a paranormal catastrophe. We could have gotten hurt or killed or possessed or…

"We need to get out of here," I hissed, remembering the soul parasite we had to pull out of Tamara. Maybe that craggy, deformed creature brought those things with it. Or maybe they burrowed into the soil like regular worms and waited for idiots like us to stumble into their lair. I should have told Aunt Astrid a protection spell cranked up to eleven would have been better than something that made me smell like candy.

"Yeah. I think you're right." Tom pulled my arm, and we started to hurry back in the direction we had come. He never let go of my hand. Not once. Not until we got into his truck.

"Well." We were both breathing hard as we sat in the cab. "You certainly are a fun date." Tom turned to me.

"Sure," I replied. "How many girls suggest trespassing on private property that is haunted or cursed or unholy? Find me an opportunity to go insane with fear, and there's no holding me back."

Tom didn't say anything but still stared at me.

"I'm sorry, Tom. I shouldn't have brought you here. I should have never suggested this, because it's way too dangerous. I should have come alone."

"What?" He looked almost hurt. "This is no place for a woman to be alone. Call me old fashioned, but it's not."

"I made you break the law."

"Your beautiful eyes can probably make me do a

lot of things, but that one I chose on my own. Sorry."

"Tom. There is something you should know about me and about my family." I took a deep breath and looked at my hands in my lap. They were dirty from the mud we'd had to crouch in. In fact, there was dirt and muck covering almost all of my left side.

"Let me guess. It has something to do with the full moon and growing hair and fangs?"

"Not quite." I laughed.

"You grow scales and a fin when you swim in salt water?"

"I'm trying to be serious." I couldn't help but chuckle. Tom scooted closer to me and stretched his right arm behind me on the seat. "You might have a different opinion of me after I tell you."

"You could tell me that Jack the Ripper was your father and Elizabeth Bathory was your mom, and none of that would change the way I feel about you."

"My mom was dragged underneath my bed when I was a little girl and disappeared. She saved me from the *thing* that was to crawl out from underneath. She died saving me from a monster."

I held my breath and continued to look at my dirty hands. Tom didn't move. I was sure he was wondering why he didn't quit while he was ahead. *Why are all the pretty ones crazy? Why didn't I ask for documentation from a shrink that this one was okay to date? How do they always know where to find me?* Yup. I was sure these were the comments going through Tom's head right now.

What was he waiting for? Where was the sarcasm? There had to be a condescending comment teetering on the tip of his tongue, just waiting to jump off.

"Well?" I spat, drawing my attitude as a cowboy draws his pistol. "I'm sure you've got something to say about it."

His face looked as if he had been slapped very hard by a stranger.

"I'm so *sorry*, Cath."

Repeating the words, he scooted even closer and pulled me to him.

I stared into his eyes and felt tears fill my own. What? Sorry? Where did that come from? How was I supposed to react to this kind of *kindness*? I did what any woman in the arms of a handsome man would do. I cried.

"I've been looking for monsters my whole life, Tom." Swallowing hard, I pulled myself together and leaned back from him slightly. "Sometimes I'm imagining them. But sometimes I run right smack into them. More than one person has left me behind because of it. I'll understand if you do too. It's not like cheering for rival baseball teams. Some things just can't be compromised."

I felt his strong hand push my head gently to his chest, where he smoothed my hair but said nothing. His heart was racing, and I figured it was because he was trying to find the right words to give me the old boot.

"I had a dream once that my mom got into a car crash." His words were soft but heavy. "I had to be about thirteen or fourteen. I told her, and she just shook it off. She drove me to school like usual, and nothing happened. But the image of her car all dented up, with steam and smoke coming from it, the windshield smashed into a spider web of glass, wouldn't leave me." He swallowed. "Finally, when I had gotten enough nerve to tell the teacher I needed to call home, the principal, Mr. Loomis, came to the classroom door and pointed at me."

I looked up and studied Tom's face. The twinkle was dulled. That was what usually happened when a person relived something sad. I tried to see if there was any indication he was lying or patronizing me. But nothing was there.

"You can imagine my reaction, right? I became hysterical. I started yelling for my mom, and Mr. Loomis told me to calm down. My mom was in the office. My father had been in an automobile accident, and she was here to take me to the hospital."

"You just saw the car in your dream?" I deduced that all on my own.

"When my mom returned home after dropping me off at school, my dad was there to change cars. It had a bigger trunk, and he needed it for something he was buying or something. I barely remember that part. I just remember seeing my mom with tears in her eyes but brave. She was always brave."

"Was your dad okay?"

"He was. Banged up, but that didn't kill him. Old age did." Tom smiled. The twinkle was back.

"Did you ever have a psychic episode after that?"

"Nothing worth mentioning. A few experiences of déjà vu. But nothing that ever made my heart stop. Well, not like that day. Oh, except for one." He snapped his fingers, nodding.

"When was that?"

"The day I first saw you."

My breath caught in my throat, and I felt the heat rise up from my toes, racing to set my cheeks ablaze.

Before I could hide my embarrassment, I felt Tom's lips against mine.

"I've been waiting all night to do that."

I clicked my tongue.

"Well, I don't know what took you so long," I teased. "We were just lying down behind a log for an infinite amount of time. What did I have to do, send up a flare or something?"

"Excuse me if a creepy old hag sniffing the dirt for our scent kept me preoccupied." Tom scooted back behind the wheel and revved the truck's engine.

"I don't think we need to worry about that now." I laughed, turning to grab my seat belt only to have my eyes captured in the milky, dead stare of the creepy old hag Tom was talking about staring in the window at us. At me!

I screamed.

"*Let me in!*" It cackled and began to scratch at the window, just as Tamara described.

"Tom! Get us out of here!"

Without a word, Tom threw the truck in drive and sped out of the speed-trap hiding place and back onto the road. In the side-view mirror, I saw the thing hobbling after us, bent yet undeterred. But it disappeared as Tom put the miles of road between it and us. You can be sure I also checked behind our seats and shined a police-issue flashlight into the flatbed through the little window to make sure there were no stowaways.

"What in heck!" Tom started to laugh as he steered the truck. It was a nervous but relieved laugh, like a balloon filled with helium and then let go. It was contagious.

When we finally pulled into my driveway, we were laughing so hard anyone who would have seen us would have testified we were drunker than skunks.

"I don't know if the phrase 'I had a wonderful time' applies to this," I teased as I climbed out of the cab.

"Right? I had an absolutely terrifying time, and I'm sure I won't sleep for a week." Tom walked around the front of the truck, took my hand, and walked me to my front door. We stood under the porch light for a few moments. "Oh, and before I forget, you'll need to give me directions to Bea's place."

"Oh yeah. They invited you for dinner. That's right." I squeezed his hand and pointed to the lovely yellow house down the block. "It's right over there. But if you get lost, you can stop by Aunt Astrid's house, and she'll give you directions." I pointed to the elegant brownstone almost directly across the street. Call me crazy, but I was pretty sure I saw a curtain fall back into place at the old girl's house. Aunt Astrid might be able to see different dimensions without being noticed, but in this dimension, she was not so stealthy.

"Well, I better be on my best behavior. They could be watching."

"Could be? I'd put money on that sure thing."

Tom turned back to me, put his finger underneath my chin, and lifted my lips to his. His lips were soft, and the kiss was gentle and proper and delightful.

"I'll see you on Friday," he said as he pulled away and headed for his truck.

"Hey, Tom? I don't think I'd tell anyone about what happened tonight. Not until we are together at my cousin's house. Is that okay?"

"No one would believe me if I did tell them." He smirked. "That I was on a date with an angel? Nope. No one will believe me. They'll have to see with their own eyes."

Just then, a dark, familiar shadow came slinking across the yard. If I'd had any doubts about Tom, they were quickly being knocked down like bricks by a wrecking ball a little at a time. It was Treacle who rubbed up against Tom's legs. Back and forth, he arched his back and pushed his head and whipped his tail around Tom, making sure he knew Treacle approved of him.

"*I think you are in love, Treacle.*"

"*If I'm not, I know someone who is,*" he said.

"See you Friday, Cath."

"Good night, Tom. Drive safe."

Libre Monstrum

❧

"You didn't say anything about your date with Tom." Aunt Astrid said as soon as I let myself in Bea's front door. "I know it was your day off at the cafe, but you wouldn't answer any of our calls or texts."

"Hello, Aunt Astrid," I said as Treacle scooted past me into the house to visit with Marshmallow, who was lounging on the sofa facing the kitchen, and Peanut Butter, who jumped down from the desk to give him a hearty welcome. I stomped up to my aunt and gave her a kiss on the cheek. "I didn't think I needed to tell you anything since you were peeking out your front window."

"That wasn't me. It was Marshmallow. Marshmallow, you sneaky kitty."

"It was her," Marshmallow told me telepathically.

"Well, I do have some things to tell you, but I want to wait until Tom arrives." I walked into the kitchen and quickly ran up to my cousin, who was busy behind the counter, chopping up something that was purple. I bumped her with my hip.

"I'm so glad you're here." She gave me a peck on the cheek.

"Where's Jake?" I asked, looking around.

"He and Blake will be here in about ten minutes. I needed some peanut oil and rice vinegar for the coleslaw salad, so the boys went to get it."

"Blake is staying for dinner, too?" Did I sound nervous?

"He is." Bea gave me a sad look. "He doesn't get home-cooked meals often, and it's important for the man watching my husband's back to know he has a little bit of family here. Even if we don't always understand each other."

"Of course, Bea." I put my hand on her shoulder. "I'm good. Speaking of good, what is that smell?"

"Savory mushroom torte in a light pastry and gravy with Asian coleslaw and homemade banana pudding for dessert."

My shoulders slumped.

"Is that all?" I teased.

"Shut up and tell us about your date."

"Well, it was fun. Interesting. And fun. And a little scary. Terrifying, really. A hint of nausea was there too."

"I think I hear wedding bells!" Aunt Astrid cried, pointing at me. "I had those same exact feelings when I met Bea's father, your uncle."

"Oh, for heaven's sake. Calm down, woman." I rolled my eyes. "Can you just tell me what I can do to help until he gets here? Then we'll spill the beans about everything. Sheesh! You're worse than first graders before summer vacation."

My aunt and cousin loved to tease me. Secretly, I loved it, too. They were the best family I could have hoped for, and the fact that they were interested in knowing Tom was comforting.

Truthfully, I would have preferred that Blake wasn't going to be with us tonight. Bea was much more caring than I was. I assumed it had to do with being able to see people's auras. It wasn't just *where* they were hurting but *how*. That nurturing side of her made her one of the most beautiful people I'd ever known.

As she chopped up the purple cabbage, she told Aunt Astrid and me about Jake's attempt at arts and crafts. Bea had wanted a wooden frame for a picture she had found of the three of us.

"I was really just thinking out loud," she said, starting to laugh. "I mumbled that it would just be a simple wooden frame. Flat. Not a lot of detail. So Jake, bless his heart, made me a Popsicle-stick frame." Tears were streaming down her cheeks as she talked. "He handed it to me before he left for work, all wrapped in tissue paper and everything."

"Daww!" I gushed.

"It was Krazy Glued together, crooked, the glue dried in a big glob at one end, and one of the sticks was stained pink from the red Popsicle it had on it. I know they have those things at the police station in the staff freezer. He ate four for the sticks!"

We were all laughing as Jake and Blake came through the door.

Jake stopped and looked at us laughing.

"You told them about my frame, didn't you?" He put his hands on his hips.

"There's no shame in not being the artsy-craftsy type, Jake," I said soothingly.

He walked over to Bea, who was still trying not to laugh, and handed her the bag of supplies she had requested.

"Hello, Detective Samberg. It's so good to see

you again." Aunt Astrid always made such a fuss over him, and I couldn't say why.

"Astrid. It's nice to see you again. Cath." He nodded.

"Hi, Blake." I smiled warily. "How are they treating you at the station?"

"Just fine," he replied. I thought it looked as if he was going to continue speaking, but not another word came from his mouth. Instead, he walked over and took a seat next to my aunt.

I didn't pursue it and turned on my designated barstool at the counter back to Bea and Jake, who were obviously whispering coded sweet nothings to one another.

When the doorbell rang, I hopped off the seat.

"No! No." Jake took my hand and motioned for me to get back on my stool. "You don't want to appear desperate. Even if you are."

"I'm going to slap you," I whispered, shaking my head. "You really are too much."

But Jake wasn't listening to me and dashed off toward the door. A hearty salutation could be heard, and as Tom appeared in the doorway, his blue jeans fitting perfectly, his proper button-down shirt tucked in, and his wavy black hair neatly combed into place,

I forgot just about everything else that had happened up to this point.

"Hi, everyone." He waved, not at all shy or nervous, unlike me. With all the cool in the world, he handed a pretty bouquet of flowers to Bea and, like a real man's man, a six-pack of something to Jake.

"I'm not really a wine person, or an alcohol person, for that matter. This is just a little concoction a friend of mine sent me from his home in Illinois." Tom took two more steps and stood next to me. "You haven't lived if you haven't tasted Green River."

"I've heard of that stuff. It's like liquefied lime-green suckers." I wrinkled my nose. Even I didn't think that sounded too appealing, and I loved junk food.

"Indeed it does." Tom slipped his arm around my waist, making me squirm. I wasn't used to any kind of public displays of affection. But he smelled so good I let him give me a gentle squeeze.

Jake and Bea thanked Tom, and within minutes, we were all enjoying Bea's mushroom tortes. Once again, I was proven wrong that a meal needed meat in order to be delicious. But the siren song of the frozen deluxe pizza in my freezer would be calling to me before the night was over.

"So Tom," Blake began as Jake and Bea began clearing away everyone's plates after dinner, "we appreciate your sending the file on the Clares to us."

"Yeah." Jake added, "We haven't had any real trouble with them, but the funny thing is we do have reports of some odd occurrences around their property."

"Like what?" Aunt Astrid looked at me.

"People have called saying they've heard scream-ing. There have been weird lights in the trees." Jake shook his head.

"But none of these have been substantiated." Blake huffed, per his usual serious self. "The reports are very random, and there haven't been any in over two years. It's my guess they are just hallucinations by people who indulged in too much alcohol. Maybe a controlled substance."

"*That is because Tamara came to the Brew Ha-Ha instead of stopping by the police station.*" I looked at Trea-cle, who slowly blinked at me before stepping over to the sliding screen door to be let out into the world again.

"*Had enough domestication?*" I smiled.

"*I'll see what's going on and report back.*"

"Stay away from the Clares' property and Evergrave Creek."

I was sure Treacle heard me, but he slipped out the door before I had even opened it all the way. After closing the door, I picked up Peanut Butter and held him in my arms.

"This stuff sounds creepy to me." He nuzzled against my chest.

"Me, too. But it gets worse."

"What do you mean?" Marshmallow, like her mistress, was a powerful cat, thoughtful and unwilling to take unnecessary risks. She looked at me, her wispy, butterfly-wing-looking ears twitching as she waited for my response.

"Tom and I went up there. To that old bridge and creek. It wasn't a smart idea."

"What happened?"

"You'll hear."

"I passed along everything I know about those people." Tom took a glass bowl of thick yellow pudding from Bea and nodded a thank you.

"Bring your dessert in the other room with us, Tom." Jake handed Blake a bowl then jerked his head in the direction of his man cave just past the kitchen.

Tom smiled, kissed me on the cheek, and headed off like a boy who was just invited to climb the rope ladder up into the best tree house on the block.

"Finally. Now we can talk," Aunt Astrid joked. "Tom is a very nice man."

"I have to say he is." I smiled. "In fact, he knows a lot more about me than, well, anyone else but you guys."

My aunt and Bea looked at each other then at me and leaned forward on the counter across and next to me as if I were quietly doling out investment advice.

"But you may not be happy about what we did."

I told my family about the date with Tom and where we ended up. By the time I got to us peeling out of the speed-trap hiding place, they were both just sitting there with their mouths open.

"So. He walked me to the door, and we said good night. And that was it."

"Oh, he's a keeper," Bea said.

"I was thinking the exact same thing," Aunt Astrid said as if she was trying not to burst out in giddy giggles.

"Don't you two have anything to say about the hag that came after us? The bridge or the area back there?"

"We'll get to that. Right now, we're talking about your love life, and that's much more important." Bea patted my hand. "You know, I didn't want to say anything, but I sensed he had a gift."

"You, too?" Aunt Astrid leaned closer to her daughter. "I didn't quite see psychic but perhaps a touch of medium in him. Maybe even channeling."

"You guys, please?" I was so embarrassed. Here I was, telling them about not just trespassing but trespassing on the haunted or cursed land of some crazies, and they were too busy picking out china patterns for me and what month I should get married. "It was only our second date."

"You're right, honey." Aunt Astrid put her hands up in front of her as if she were stopping an oncoming train. "We do need to address the concerns at hand. I found something you both might find interesting."

My aunt shuffled over to her purse, scratching Marshmallow behind the ears as she did so, and came back to the counter with a piece of paper. When she finally unfolded it, I was surprised it covered almost half the counter like a tablecloth.

"I had to make photocopies of this at the library and tape them together. But it looks pretty good to me," Aunt Astrid said while she smoothed out what was an old map of Wonder Falls and the surrounding Wonder Falls unincorporated.

"This has got to be at least fifty years old. I don't recognize half these streets." Bea ran her finger over the wrinkled paper and squinted at the names.

"This little beauty was tucked away in the local history section of the library," Aunt Astrid said.

The map my aunt spread out in front of us was from, in fact, almost seventy-five years ago. It showed all of Wonder Falls Proper as well as the unincorporated sections, neighboring townships, and even some small patches of uncharted acreage.

"Funny that Archie Jones's property didn't just border the huge mass of land the Clares own, but it was encircled by it." She pointed to the small area on the map that we had visited in person the other day. "Why would a farmer buy that many acres but have a tiny section they technically didn't pay for? It makes no sense unless that land isn't there."

"Your mom has been hitting the bottle again, hasn't she?" I leaned over toward Bea, shaking my head in disgust.

"No. Smoking funny cigarettes," Bea joked. "Mom. How can that be? You were there. You and Cath. And Cath and her knight in shining armor were just there. And the police found Archie's body, so they were there. There is land there."

"There is the illusion of land there. Girls..." Aunt

Astrid's face became grave, and the wrinkles around her mouth and eyes became like dark cuts in her skin. "Something is hiding there. Something that isn't afraid, because its caretakers allow it."

"So you're saying the Clares are keeping some kind of paranormal pet?" I had forgotten about my banana pudding and quickly began to devour the tasty dessert.

"Well, a pet can be controlled. I am thinking that it might be the other way around. The Clares are kept by this being." My aunt shook her head as she went back to her purse on the couch and returned with one of her books.

"*Libre Monstrum.*" She handed the book to Bea. "*The Book of Monsters.* It's an older edition and doesn't have everything. But it might have what we are looking for."

Bea opened it to a page with a horrific ink drawing of a catlike creature eating the eyes of what looked like a corpse.

"Really?" I said and set the remaining bit of pudding down on the counter. My stomach didn't want any more. "What is that?"

"A Feline Eye Eater. See also Canine Eye Eater," Bea read aloud. Hand that girl a book, and she was instantly transported back to school, devouring page after page of information and ready to take a quiz designed to stump Einstein. If there were any kind of answer between the pages of this hardcover, Bea would find it and become an expert at paranormal monsters in the process.

"Now, we had an encounter with a soul parasite. They are in there. Cath, maybe you'll see something about that hag in there."

"Do I really have to look through all the pictures?" I cringed at the thought.

"I'll look for anything that fits your description and show you," Bea offered. "That way you don't have to see everything. I'll weed out the gross stuff."

"Thanks, Bea. That'll work."

But before we could get too far into the project at hand, the Three Musketeers came waltzing back into the kitchen.

"Bea, taste this stuff." Jake smiled, handing her an almost empty bottle of Green River. Tom smiled as he watched. "You were a kid once. This will send you all the way back there."

Bea quickly picked up the book and tucked it underneath the counter next to *101 Vegan Recipes* and *Eat Healthy, Eat Vegetarian*. She may have been a vegan and helped all of us eat a little healthier, but one thing she wasn't was rude. She took the bottle, gave the opening a quick sniff, and without hesitation tipped the end up, getting a healthy gulp of the green liquid in her mouth. After swallowing, she licked her lips.

"That tastes like those baby suckers we used to get as kids with the loop for the stick." She smiled as the taste brought back memories of the two of us as little girls.

"We used to get those from the drug store for a couple pennies," I remembered. I'd drunk Green River on occasion. It seemed to be the perfect accompaniment for a cheeseburger with everything. My stomach growled even though I just ate.

"Well, I hate to break up the party, but Blake and I have to get back to the station." Jake kissed Bea on the cheek and mussed my hair as if I were a kid. "Looks like there has been a next of kin located for Mr. Archie Jones. We need to ask them some questions and go through all the formalities. But they are hailing from South Carolina. I doubt we are going to come up with anything helpful."

Blake turned to Tom, and I saw him extend his hand. The two men shook hands, exchanging a few pleasantries as Tom smiled broadly and Blake looked serious and straight and uptight like usual.

"Bea, the meal was delicious." Blake waved as he

backed toward the door. "Aunt Astrid, Cath, it's always nice to see you." He said those last words looking at me, but I didn't think it meant anything. Right?

"Just wait one second, Blake. My holster is upstairs." Jake turned. Across from the kitchen in the small hallway between the family room and the kitchen was a flight of stairs that led to the three bedrooms on the second floor. Jake disappeared up the steps, followed by an excited Peanut Butter, leaving Blake standing there waiting.

"Bea, I'll have to be leaving soon, too. I've got the eleven-to-seven shift for the next three nights. A little bit of overtime comes in handy," Tom said, and he was looking at me. "But can you point me to the bathroom?"

"Sure, just follow me," Bea said, leading him around the foyer to the guest powder room.

Aunt Astrid turned and lazily began to stroke Marshmallow, and I was left to make things comfortable for the guy who went to great lengths to do the opposite for me.

"How are you and Darla doing?" I asked before I could stop myself. Did I even want to know? No. I didn't want to know anything about him or the woman who took every chance to make my high school career a hell on earth. She had opted to continue that route in adulthood as well.

"We decided to part ways." Blake rocked back on his heels. I couldn't tell if he was sad or happy or indifferent. All of his expressions seemed the same.

"I'm sorry to hear that." *NOT!* "You guys looked happy."

Yes, my heart felt a twinge of satisfaction. I knew it was childish, but I didn't care. Wasn't it interesting that when Tom and I started seeing each other, suddenly Blake and Darla weren't seen hanging on each other around town? Okay, to be fair, Blake never hung on Darla, but she sure as anything hung on him like a tacky, moth-ridden, cheap coat.

"She's a lovely girl. Just not what I'm looking for."

"Oh" was all I could say as I looked at his face. There was something there. I wasn't just saying it, letting my ego go wild with delight over his breakup. For a split second, it looked as though he was about to say something, but my aunt Astrid interrupted. I had forgotten she was there.

"Detective, please join us again next week for dinner. We just love having you," she cooed. I turned and looked at her with raised eyebrows. "Don't we, Cath."

My sarcastic side wanted to jump right out and give Blake a verbal slap that knocked him to the ground. But before that clever retort could fully form in my head, I uttered this instead...

"Yes. We do love having you."

It wasn't a lie. Sure, things didn't work out between us. Just because Darla wasn't what he was looking for didn't mean I was. He couldn't accept my being a witch. It frightened him, even if somewhere deep down he was attracted to me.

At that moment, Tom appeared from around the corner with that fantastic smile and wearing those jeans.

Marshmallow stood from her perch on the sofa by Aunt Astrid and quickly ascended the arm of the chair and higher up to the back, meowing in Tom's direction. As if he understood every syllable, he walked over and began to scratch the feline affectionately under the chin.

"You're like catnip," I teased. "You should see Treacle come running from three blocks away to rub on him."

"I like animals," he said, leaning down to look in Marshmallow's face and receive a head-butt of approval. "But I do have to go. Mind walking me to my truck?" He looked at me and gave me a wink.

He reached for my hand, and I took his, still feeling a little weird about the affectionate gestures but getting more and more used to them.

"Be careful out there, Blake," I said as I walked past him.

"You, too," he mumbled.

Once outside, I quickly pulled my hand away and folded my arms in front of me.

"My gosh, it sure did get cold." I shivered. "I thought I'd just need a sweater. Looks like I'll be running home tonight. It's too cold to walk."

"I have something for you," Tom said, hurrying to his truck and opening the driver's-side door. "I saw it the other day at a little antique shop not far from my place. It reminded me of you."

Tom handed me a small white box about the size of a silver dollar. When I opened it up, I found a brooch. A black-and-gold Art Deco–style frame around a bright-green emerald cut piece of glass. It was dazzling.

"See?" He took it out of the box. "It's a green stone. Get it?"

I nodded but didn't find any words forming in there.

"Do you like it?"

"I love it. It's the most beautiful thing anyone's ever given to me."

I guessed Tom didn't have any more words forming in his head either, because he didn't say anything else. Instead, he just took a step toward me, slipped his arms around my waist, and kissed me. I no longer felt the cold.

Otto Clare

❧❀❧

After dinner at Bea's, I was feeling wonderful even though by the time I left, we hadn't identified what it was lurking in the Clare property that scared the dickens out of me. Bea had yet to spot a milky-eyed hag in Aunt Astrid's book. Despite Aunt Astrid suggesting the property Tom and I trespassed on may not even really be there, I still had a spring in my step.

Yes, I will admit that the juvenile part of me that sometimes reared its ugly head was making a brief appearance and gloating over the breakup between Blake and Darla. But I couldn't be sure it was all Blake's idea. Perhaps he wanted to stay with Darla, and she, being the selfish creature that she was, didn't think he was good enough for her. That would be just like Darla. If that was the case, it was best Blake find out for himself. He never would have believed me had I been the one to tell him.

However, if *he* broke up with *her*, that would satisfy my desire for revenge on her. It was certainly better than the hex of incurable scalp pimples I wanted to put on her. But my aunt would know it was me who did it and put a binding spell on me until death.

The real reason for my happiness was the brooch Tom gave me. After I got home that night, I tore into my closet, looking for something to wear with it, and realized I had nothing.

Such a special object deserved a special getup, so for the first time in several months, I decided to head to the fashion strip of Wonder Falls.

About twenty miles from the Brew-Ha-Ha was an area of town that was loaded with not just regular shops like Macy's and Bloomingdale's but also high-end consignment shops, vintage thrift stores, and good, old-fashioned secondhand stores. I was determined to find something beautiful to wear with this brooch.

It looked great on my pea coat, but I wanted something else. The stone in the middle was at least an inch wide and glowed a luxurious forest green that reminded me of the flowing velvet gown Scarlett O'Hara made from her mother's curtains.

So in order to find something as unique as the pin, I stopped in the consignment store first. It was as if the planets had aligned especially for me and said, "Cath is going shopping. Make sure she gets exactly what she wants."

Right there, at the front of the Busy Bee Consignment shop, was a luxurious, baggy, green crumpled-velvet sweater with small cuffs and a drop waist. It was fantastic. I envisioned myself strolling into the Brew-Ha-Ha in this sweater and black slacks, or dare I look to my left and purchase the stylish yet over-the-top leather pencil skirt on display?

It wasn't surprising that I spent over an hour picking through every display and rack in the shop, gasping over the beautifully impractical clothes and debating if it really was necessary to own a pair of leopard-print stiletto heels and matching sixties-style hot pants. I needed to wear something to the grocery store, right?

But I kept my head about me and bought just the sweater. It was enough. It was beautiful. And when I got in my car and took the brooch off my coat and put it against the fabric of the sweater, I gasped. It looked just as I'd hoped. It was romantic and stylish and glamorous. There wasn't much need for this kind of decadence in my life. I had simple tastes, and although I preferred my vintage cardigans and Converse All-Star gym shoes, this was different. This was my way of showing Tom how much I appreciated his gift. I wanted to feel as beautiful as this antique pin was, as beautiful as the gesture to buy it for me was, and as beautiful as Tom was.

When I started my car and got back on the expressway to head home, you can imagine how I was knocked off guard seeing an all-too-familiar truck barreling down on me from at least nine or ten car lengths back.

For a minute, I thought I was seeing things. But as I tried to watch in the rearview mirror and keep my eyes on the road in front of me, I saw the beat-up black truck weaving from lane to lane, passing cars and honking the horn.

Bracing for an epic episode of road rage, I gripped the steering wheel tightly as the truck maneuvered itself alongside of me.

Looking to my right, I saw the driver was not the younger, bald Clare who chased my aunt and me off his property but rather the creepy older gentleman who ordered us to leave.

He paid no attention to me, and instead of

running me off the road as I had envisioned, he swerved ahead of me, around a Cadillac, nearly cut off a Honda, and left a Chevy Bolt in the dust. That wasn't really hard to do.

Without thinking, I hit the accelerator and gave chase.

Now, I knew there was proper protocol for tailing a car. I'd seen enough Humphrey Bogart and James Cagney movies to get the general gist of the method. But putting one or two cars in between us was hard. So I threw caution to the wind and got behind the truck, keeping a safe distance of two car lengths between us.

I began to wonder where he was coming from. It wasn't the fashion strip. I was pretty sure of that. There was nothing in the bed of his truck. The dirt and grime was crusted and dry, so I didn't think he was mudding or doing anything recreational like that.

Wherever he'd been, he was in a hurry to get back. We were getting closer and closer to town, and still he had yet to ease up on the accelerator. The speed limit signs that read forty miles an hour were being passed up at sixty. I prayed no one would pull out in front of me or a random baby stroller would somehow manage to blow into the street.

A huge sigh of relief came from me when I finally saw the red taillights and the left turn signal go off. He turned into the Wonder Falls Animal Clinic. I brought Treacle here to Dr. Fields for his yearly boosters.

"What in the world?" I muttered. This was an odd place to be speeding to. I let him pull into the parking lot, drove up another block, made a U-turn, and came back just in time to see the old Clare stomping up to the front door. He yanked it open and disappeared inside as I slowly pulled into the lot. There was an open parking spot next to the truck, but I didn't think it wise to take such a bold risk. Instead, I found one at the corner of the lot, backed in, and waited.

I shut the car off and felt the air inside start to get cold almost immediately. It was a chilly, overcast day, and when I took a deep breath of fresh air, I thought it smelled as if rain might be coming.

Finally, after twenty minutes of waiting, I saw Otto Clare emerge with a scowl on his face. He had no animal with him, thank heavens. But I did see him stuff something into his pocket. Could there be animals at his farm? The idea broke my heart.

I watched as Otto Clare peeled out of the parking

lot, heading in the direction of town. Within seconds, he was completely out of view.

I got out of my car and, rubbing my cold hands together, made my way to the entrance of the vet's office. The warm office and the sound of a couple of barking dogs soothed my nerves.

The receptionist, Bunny McFadden, came waddling up from the back of the office.

"Hey, Cath." She waved a pleasant hello. Her figure was full and mostly bosom that supported her double chin. She always wore one of those cute nurses' tops with puppies or kitties or hearts or "I HEART my vet" on them. I had been seeing her behind the front desk for over five years now. "Is Treacle all right?"

"Hi, Bunny. Yes, he's fine. Out snooping around the neighborhood like usual."

"He's up to date on everything, isn't he?" She quickly plopped down in her receptionist chair and rolled herself backward to the seven-drawer file cabinet behind her. Before I could say anything, she had his file in her hand. "Looks like he'll need a checkup in another two months. I'll make sure to send you a reminder. Wonder Falls has got bats, and they carry rabies."

She winked at me, wrinkling up her already pug-like nose and waving a manicured hand in my direction.

"That would be great."

"Other than that, he's good?" She quickly typed something into her computer and stuck the file in a bin marked To Be Filed.

"Yeah. Just out prowling during the day but indoors most nights."

"Don't you wish you knew what they were up to all day long? If only they could talk." Bunny smiled cutely again.

I just smiled back.

"So what can I do for you?" She finally scooted her chair underneath her desk and looked up at me.

"That man that just came in here. Can I ask what he wanted?"

"What man?"

"The man who just came in. His last name is Clare." I leaned against the counter, shifting from my right leg to my left. I watched as Bunny shook her head.

"No one came in here." She was so sure.

Just then, Dr. Fields came down the hallway, holding a folder underneath his arm as he wrapped his left index finger with a Band-Aid.

"Hello, Cath," he said, looking up then down at

his finger then up at me again. He was a pleasant older man with a stocky build and a contagious smile. "Hamsters aren't always as nice as they pretend to be. Treacle okay?"

"Yeah." I scratched my head. "I just saw a neighbor of mine come in and then leave right away, and I was just wondering what he was in for." I heard the words, and they sounded normal to me, but the look on Dr. Fields's face as well as Bunny's face made me feel as if I'd just asked to do a tap dance with my pet potato.

"He was in this morning?" the doctor asked.

"Just now."

"You are the only one who has come in all morning, Cath." Dr. Fields smiled politely.

There was no point in arguing. I knew what I saw, but here were two people who had no dog in the race, no pun intended, who were both telling me they had seen no one come in this morning. No one but me.

"I'm sorry. I must have been seeing things," I joked nervously. "I could have sworn I saw his truck pull in, but maybe I didn't," I lied. I knew what I had seen, and Otto Clare had stomped into the vet's clinic then, twenty minutes later, stomped out. Twenty minutes! "You know, while I'm here, I may as well schedule Treacle's next appointment since he's due."

I took the little card from Bunny that read "No Bones About It! It's time for your checkup" with a picture of a mutt and a calico nuzzling each other on it.

"We'll see you in two months," Bunny chimed, smiling happily.

"Yeah, great. Thanks, guys, and have a great day."

As I was walking out of the office, I rolled my eyes up and saw it. There it was, just staring at me. A security camera. Now it was my turn to smile.

Trespassing on Otto's land could be brushed off as a mistake, even with a police officer as my accomplice. But breaking and entering was something different altogether. I wouldn't be telling Tom about this.

Atropa Belladonna

❧

Calmly, I got in my car and drove home, changed into my new sweater, with my brooch and a pair of skinny black jeans that looked better with the loose baggy sweater than with anything else. A little red lipstick was added as a final touch, and I headed over to the café for my shift.

Now, if I didn't feel good when I put on my new duds, I certainly did when I stepped into the café, only to see Darla Castellano. The woman was sitting by herself, typing on her cell phone with her long, manicured fingers, making an annoying *click-click-click* as she messaged and/or tweeted or whatever she was doing. If I had to guess, I would have said it was probably an arsenal of selfies.

"My gosh, Cath." Bea clapped her hands together and bounced on her heels. "You look beautiful."

"Where did you get that beautiful brooch?" Aunt Astrid asked, standing from her favorite seat, where she was organizing some of the morning receipts. I told her and Bea the whole story about Tom giving it to me yesterday and that I didn't want to wear it until I found a nice sweater to wear it with. Out of the corner of my eye, I saw Darla leaning closer to hear what I was saying. She thought she was so sly.

"It looks like they were made to go together," my aunt gushed. "I hope you'll let me borrow that sometime. I know just the hat it would look perfect on."

I smiled but then froze.

"You don't mean that blue turban, do you?" Bea spoke before I could. My aunt sometimes went a little overboard with her adventures in accessories. The blue turban she had was one of those "DON'Ts" you see in magazines all the time.

"Mom, you look like Johnny Carson when you wear that thing."

"You're crazy," my aunt snapped. "I look like an exotic fortune teller from Transylvania."

"Maybe from Portage County across the river," I teased. Portage County was a sleepy Mayberry kind of town where the most exciting thing in the past year was the induction of a five-hundred-pound sow in the *Guinness Book of World Records* for most piglets born. Twenty-four.

"Oh, you think you're so smart." My aunt laughed.

As I laughed, I went behind the counter, grabbed my apron and a slice of pumpkin pie, and took a big bite before telling Bea and Aunt Astrid I had something new to share with them.

"It's interesting you say that, because I spent the night looking through Mom's *Libre Monstrum*, and I narrowed it down to two possible suspects." Bea pulled a piece of paper out of her pocket. There were notes in her impeccable script written on it. "It could be a tertius harpy."

"Tertius harpy!" I snapped my fingers. "Why didn't I think of that? What is it?"

"I thought you'd never ask," Bea teased, knowing full well I had no idea what she was referring to. "Tertius harpies are creatures that tag along with other, more dominant entities and wreak their havoc on the leftovers. They aren't a huge threat, nor are they particularly bright. But they can cause extreme terror to anyone unfamiliar with or unwilling to believe in the paranormal. They can also cause physical problems like nausea, headache, loss of appetite, and irritable bowel syndrome. If not treated, the symptoms will usually go away on their own."

"So if that was just a toady to a greater entity… what is the greater entity?" I asked while grabbing two oatmeal raisin cookies from the cookie container behind the counter.

"I'm not so sure this was a toady." Bea looked down at her notes. "Based on your description, this one fit the bill. I thought if the land we are talking about isn't really there but is a psychic illusion or perhaps a little plot from another dimension, this tertius harpy may just be along for the ride and roams around the small bit of property, scaring anyone who comes by. That is what I was hoping."

"But?" Aunt Astrid took a step closer.

"But then I came across the Rotmirage."

My shoulders slumped, and I rolled my eyes.

"I don't like the sound of that," I whispered, shaking my head.

"Then you'll hate this." Bea leaned in closer to me as Aunt Astrid took a seat on the stool across from us and rested her chin in her palm as she listened. "A Rotmirage is a low-level demon. It can't come to this dimension by itself. It has to be summoned. Once it is summoned, it remains with whoever called it, doing their bidding."

"Demons are greedy things," Aunt Astrid said. "It wouldn't do this for free. What does it get in return?"

"That depends on who summoned it." Bea folded up her notes and put them back in her pocket. "From what I read, it will accept sanity, physical health, eyesight, certain emotions, animal essence, or the family members of the summoner as payment. It will take a little at a time so the unfortunate soul who called this thing will barely notice any payment has been deducted. They have to squint to read the paper, so what. They keep forgetting what they started to do, no big deal. But as they get what they are asking for, they become more and more addicted to the demon. They don't want to give up what they've got. So they let it sink its talons in further and further until there is no getting out of this thing's grip."

"Do you think the Clares summoned this thing?" I asked, feeling my blood pressure rise at the thought of them using animals to fuel some demon that shouldn't even be here.

"Yes. The worst part is they think they control it." Bea took a deep breath. "It is controlling them. Cath, I don't know what would have happened had you not cast that protection spell. This is a dirty, low-down demon. The Clares are not much better."

"That would explain the suicides at the bridge. The victims may not have been suicidal at all when they walked into the woods." Aunt Astrid kneaded a paper napkin in her hand. I handed her a cookie, which she accepted and bit into. "But if the Clares requested help from the Rotmirage, it would take its payment from any unsuspecting person within its property line."

"Jeez. It sounds like you and I narrowly escaped the Clare farm the other day," I said to my aunt, who agreed with a mouth full of cookie.

It seemed as good a time as any, so I told the story of what happened earlier, from my fear on the expressway of being run down by Otto Clare all the way until I walked out of the Wonder Falls Animal Clinic after being told no such man had entered or exited the building.

"I'm telling you, as sure as I'm standing here, I saw that fellow go in the vet's office and come out twenty minutes later, stuffing something into his pocket." I picked up the wedge of pie and took a giant bite, wiping the crumbs and half my lipstick off. "What do you guys think? Are you up for an adventure?"

It didn't take much coercing.

After closing the café for the night, we went down in the bunker and discussed our options.

"We might just have to break in." I shrugged as if this were no big deal. "Aunt Astrid, if you could put a time-stop spell on the building, we could go in and out without tripping the alarm. It wouldn't go off until Bunny and the doc arrived there in the morning."

"You're such a rebel," Bea said admiringly.

"We don't want to do that." Aunt Astrid pursed her lips. "We go in without disturbing anything, or we don't go. Now, what I was thinking will require a bit of effort on your parts and may make you very sick for the next couple of days."

"Burnout or another kind of sick?"

"Another kind of sick," she stated seriously and proceeded to tell us her plan.

By the time the sun had set, we were sure the animal clinic was closed. The autumn air was turning colder and colder over the past few days, and tonight, I was glad I brought mittens and a scarf, even if they had green-and-yellow stripes and there were tassels on the ends of both. The biggest decision we had to make was who was going to drive, and as usual, it turned out to be me because I drive better than Bea.

"Oh, you do not," she whined from the backseat.

"I do so. You drive like an old lady."

"Okay, Mario Andretti. If I were you, I'd pull this bucket of bolts around the back so any traffic going by won't notice us."

"Good call." I turned down the side street, and even though there wasn't an official road behind the veterinary office, there was a large dirt patch that was hard and hidden by a couple of bushes.

There was a wire fence at the back of the clinic where an auto dealership had taken up a good bit of land for rows and rows of good deals on new and used cars.

"Maybe I should park down there?" I pointed. "No one would notice another car."

"No, but they might notice a clunker next to all those shiny deals. It would stick out more than it does here," Bea thought out loud. She did have a point.

Finally, we all looked at each other and decided to get started.

First we checked to make sure there were no lights on other than the emergency lights on the inside. No one was burning the midnight oil.

"Okay. It looks deserted. I'm ready. You ready?" I looked at Bea.

"I'm ready. Mom?"

Aunt Astrid stood next to the rear exit door. Planting her feet firmly about a foot apart, she withdrew from her pocket three berries of atropa belladonna. They were poisonous.

"You girls understand what to do?" she asked us for the sixth time since we left the café.

We both nodded. Although it was my nature to make sarcastic and inappropriate remarks, I followed my well-mannered cousin's lead and kept my mouth shut.

"Put the berry under your tongue." She handed one to Bea and one to me. "Join hands." I took hold of Bea's hand with one hand and Aunt Astrid's with the other.

"Don't let go until I say so."

My aunt began her incantation. I hadn't heard this one before. The words were unfamiliar, and I wasn't even sure if she was speaking English. They began to blend together in a muffled way, as if I were listening to a couple arguing in the room next door.

The next thing to go was my vision. It didn't go exactly, but things began to slow down and speed up. We were treading as if we were underwater, yet the trees and bushes were furiously whipping around us as though a tornado had touched down.

Before I could ask anything, I felt my aunt's grip tighten around my hand as she pulled Bea and me toward the door. Closer and closer we came to it, until I blinked and my aunt was gone except for her arms. They were sticking out of the metal exit door, holding on to Bea and me. I tightened my grip, and I felt her pull again and watched as my hands disappeared into the door. I couldn't see them, and I could only feel the strange sensation of cold metal against my skin, around my skin, even inside my skin.

I looked at Bea, whose eyes were wide, showing how scared she was. I gripped her hand tighter and squeezed my eyes shut as one final yank pulled us through. It was like doing a belly flop. A hard yet pliable surface hit me, then I passed into it, feeling it all around me. My breath was held tightly in my chest. I didn't dare open my eyes. Had I been with anyone else, I would have freaked out and screamed, letting the metal or wood or whatever it was seep into my mouth and fill my eyes. But I concentrated on the hands I was holding. I had grown up holding these hands. I could tell Bea's hands from a million others. They were soft yet firm. Like how I'd assume an artist's hands would feel from molding clay or maneuvering a paintbrush. Aunt Astrid's were bonier. They were hard from mixing potions and burning sage and handling heavy books.

But as soon as I calmed down, a fresh wave of fear washed over me until I heard her.

"You're okay, Cath. Open your eyes."

It couldn't be.

"Mom?" I cried out, afraid to open my eyes. Afraid of where I had passed into.

"It's your aunt, honey. Open your eyes. You're okay."

My eyes fluttered open, and I realized I was flat on my back inside a dark room. Bea was to my left, holding a small trash can up to her face as she vomited. I didn't feel nauseous. But my head was pounding to beat the band.

"Did we just pass through that door?"

"Yes." Aunt Astrid helped me sit up, and my head swam. She put her hand underneath my chin and ordered me to spit. I spit out the berry. It left a bitter taste in my mouth. "Bea, honey? You all right?"

"Right as rain, Mom." She hurled pitifully. "Just need a minute."

I rubbed my head.

"I don't need to know how you did that," I grumbled. "I don't ever want to do it again."

"We still have to go back. But let's get what we came here for."

I got to my feet and went over to Bea. Extending my hand down to her, I helped her to her feet and watched as she pulled the bag from the can and dropped it in the biohazard disposal. No one would find it.

With the camera in plain view of the door, we followed the cable with a pen flashlight I swiped from the doc's office. It led to a closet at the back of the office not far from where we had entered.

Thankfully, it wasn't locked, and we all let out a sigh of relief.

"I don't think I could have passed through that door too," I muttered as I turned the knob.

There it was. Above a metal shelving unit stacked with towels, boxes of rubber gloves, bags of cat litter, and old newspapers was an old television hooked to a VCR.

"I'll say another thank heavens that the doc isn't high tech." I grabbed a step stool and proceeded to press the buttons on the machine. Yes, there was a tape in there. Yes, it looked as if it had recorded.

"Okay. I'm going to rewind it a bit and see what we get."

There was no way of telling if what we were

watching was before or after I came into the office. The only thing we could do was rewind the entire thing and sit and watch it all. I grabbed a folding chair for Aunt Astrid, and Bea wheeled Bunny's chair back. I sat on the step stool. The screen was cut up into four areas—the front door, the room with the animals and supplies, the back door, and finally, the doctor's office.

My head was still hurting, and I could tell from Bea's complexion that she wasn't feeling well, either. The only one who looked good was Aunt Astrid.

"I'm hungry," she muttered.

The thought of food made my head throb and sent Bea dashing back to the small bucket.

"Better keep that with you," I called, wincing as my teasing caused me more pain in my head.

Finally, I saw myself on the screen. It was a grainy black-and-white image, but we all could tell it was me.

"He came in just before me." I hit Rewind and gritted my teeth as the flashing and ribbons of black and white assaulted my eyes. "There!" I panted. It was him. Otto Clare. He walked in as though he owned the place. What did he do? Why didn't anyone else see him? Bunny was right there at the desk! He walked right past her!

"What did he want? He went into the doctor's office and…" I rubbed my pounding head and snapped my fingers. "The drugs are kept there."

Sure enough, Otto Clare went up to the medicine cabinet and began to help himself, filling a bag he had pulled out from his pocket.

"Guys." Bea wobbled back to the closet door, holding the trash can in her arm. "There's something outside."

"So now we know where the horse tranquilizers came from," I muttered through my veil of pain.

"Guys? Did you hear what I said?" Bea put her hand on my shoulder to steady herself. "There's something outside."

"Something or someone?" I asked, squinting.

"Some*thing*," she whispered. "Listen."

When I heard it, my heart turned to ice in my chest.

"Where are you? Let me in. Let me in."

Rotmirage

"What is that thing doing here? This isn't on Clare property!" I hissed, hoping it couldn't hear through the walls.

"Oh dear." Aunt Astrid was the only one of us not suffering from some kind of ill effect of travelling through solid matter. "I wonder if it can move through objects, too."

"If it could, I think I would have seen it in the forest, right?" I asked, hoping my aunt would give me a nod and a sigh of relief. Instead, she had an expression similar to one that said, "Sorry, but I accidentally burnt your house down."

"What is it doing?" Bea held a tissue to her lips and nearly gagged on the words she was saying.

"It's trying to get in the same way we did." Aunt Astrid was staring at the back door we had passed through. Her vision of other dimensions was telling her something. Then I heard it and knew what was happening.

"Oh no. It's digging for a way in." I could hear the Rotmirage scratching and clawing at the door, as it had at the window of Tom's truck and Tamara's car.

"It knows we passed through there," my aunt whispered. "Any minute, it's going to pass through the same seam we slipped through."

"How can that be?" Bea asked as she stiffened her back. I saw her trying to pull herself together to help, but it was a struggle. I knew the feeling. My head was pounding so hard I could feel it in my gums.

"I think it can see it. Like I can." Aunt Astrid stood up and walked dangerously close to the door. "I see the split in the part through the dimensions. It's coming in here. There's no stopping it now."

That singsongy voice that was a twisted and diseased version of a child's voice was becoming clearer and clearer from the other side of the door. Its frantic scratching was relentless. Any other being would have bloody stumps by now. But what did I know? Maybe its fingers were bloody but that didn't matter. Maybe it was using those gnarled claws and gnawing at the door with its teeth, too. All I knew was that any second, that hideous thing was going to push itself through the solid door and I'd be staring into those milky-white eyes again.

"We can't just stand here." Bea set her bucket down and looked around. Without hesitating, she pulled the fire extinguisher off the wall. There was a yardstick against the wall and a stapler on the small table in the corner. I took one in each hand and joined my cousin, standing in front of Aunt Astrid. Before we could launch our ruthless assault, I heard another sound that made my heart break.

"Meeeooooow!"

I dropped my "weapons" and dashed to the small window on the left side of the door we all passed through. Yanking the blinds up, I looked out. My eyes suddenly filled with tears. It was Treacle.

His black fur was standing straight up, making him look at least twice his size. With an arched back and raised tail, he hissed and growled at the Rotmirage as fiercely as any lion would toward a hyena.

The Rotmirage stopped its frantic scratching and

whirled around to face my cat. It crouched down and leaned on the tops of its curled claws and obscenely bounced on its haunches.

But Treacle didn't back down. I didn't know if the Rotmirage understood what my cat was saying, but it couldn't mistake his tone. It growled and peeled its lips back from its teeth, licking them as a hungry dog would.

"No." I could barely find my voice. "I've got to help him."

Aunt Astrid took hold of my arm and held it tightly. She saw something.

"What's he doing?" I began to cry. "Aunt Astrid, what do you see?"

She shook her head but said nothing.

Before I could charge for the door and yank it open, Treacle jumped at the Rotmirage. His green eyes were wide. His mouth was open, baring every tooth he had. Every claw was extended. He was ready for battle and took it right to the face and neck of the Rotmirage. When he landed, I could see him sink his claws and fangs deep into the flesh of the creature. A howl like nothing I had ever heard in my life filled my ears, and my disgust and terror made my skin ripple.

I watched as it grabbed my cat and tore him from its face and neck, leaving deep wounds that oozed and bubbled. With enough force to rattle the frame, it threw Treacle into the door it was trying to get into and disappeared.

As if reading my mind, my aunt took both Bea and me by the hand, and we were wrenched through the door without it or anything else being disturbed.

My head felt as if it had been pounded with a mallet. Bea had fallen to her knees and was throwing up again. With blurry eyes, I looked and saw Treacle. He was on the ground, not moving. Quickly, I knelt down and scooped him into my arms. Instantly, his purring machine whirred into action.

"Oh, thank God." I sobbed, pulling the cat close to my face, holding him like a newborn baby, close and tightly to my chest.

"Let's get out of here." Aunt Astrid touched my shoulder. She was nervously looking around.

I stood and went to Bea, offering her my elbow to use to steady herself and get up. We hurried to my car. I handed Treacle off to Aunt Astrid, who gently stroked his head. Bea, who fell into the backseat and was drenched in sweat, reached a hand up to touch him.

"He'll be okay, Cath. There is nothing attached to him or any broken bones. Bruises, maybe," she whispered before lying down on the backseat with her arms over her stomach.

I rubbed my aching head and let out a sigh of relief.

"What do we do now?" I started the engine and, without a look back, gunned my little car as fast as it would go, kicking up dirt and gravel behind me as I left the Wonder Falls Veterinary Clinic behind.

"I need to get home," Bea mumbled. "I think some chamomile-and-mint tea might do the trick."

"You better do the same, Cath. Get this kitty some milk, and both of you go right to bed."

"You're not going to get an argument from me." I looked in the rearview mirror, expecting to see the Rotmirage hobbling after us, but there was nothing.

Every street light and stoplight along the way home felt like a searchlight shining right in my eyes, making my head hurt. We drove in silence, although all of us were thinking the same thing. How did that thing find us? How did Otto Clare get in and out of the veterinary office with drugs and no one seeing him? And what in the world was he doing with those drugs?

None of us were in any condition to discuss the

night's events. Except maybe Aunt Astrid, who was alert and still hungry. She said so as we drove past a Taco Bell, making me shudder at the thought of all those bright fluorescent lights and poor Bea groan at the idea of fast food. Actually, Bea always groaned at the idea of fast food on account of the additives and such. But this was a sickened groan at the idea of any kind of food. The poor girl was in bad shape.

"How about it? Do you want some milk when we get home?" I looked quickly at Treacle then back at the road.

"Yes. That would be nice." He waved the tip of his tail at me lazily. The speedometer needle showed I was going ten miles over the limit. I wanted to be home as badly as everyone else.

Once at Bea's house, I watched my cousin pull herself out of the backseat.

"It's been fun, girls." She waved as if she were drunk and hurried to her front door. Once inside, she turned, waved quickly, and slammed the door shut behind her.

I dropped off my aunt and waited until she was also safely inside before driving across the street to my home. I picked Treacle up from the passenger seat and held him like a baby over my shoulder as we got inside. The cold fall air, the slight breeze, even the stars in the black sky made my head pulse painfully.

"A little milk for you and some aspirin for me."

Treacle purred happily as we entered the house and I gently closed the door and locked it behind us.

Enzo

❧❧❧

"How in the world did you know we were at the vet's office?" I asked, pouring Treacle's milk by candlelight. It might as well have been a blazing inferno, minus the heat, the way the tiny flame hurt my eyes.

"I stopped by to see Marshmallow. She told me where you guys were headed. I knew you were going to need help."

I set the small saucer of milk on the counter in front of him.

"How did you know that?"

Treacle looked up, licking his whiskers, and backed up on his haunches to sit and groom his paws. His green eyes looked at me intensely.

"I heard it from Enzo. He's a stray and a survivor of the Clare Farm."

My heart ached at those words.

"He was there?"

"Yes. And that creature."

"The Rotmirage?"

"If that's what you call it. It's picked up on your scent. Tom's too. It won't forget until it's gotten to you both."

"Did it follow my scent to the vet's office?"

"It did. But it couldn't figure out how you got in. Lucky for you I showed up."

That was the truth. I don't want to imagine what would have happened to all of us had that thing gotten in. Treacle continued to tell me more.

The Rotmirage fed on energy from mammals. Plant life or fish didn't do anything for it. That would've been like dropping in a grain of sand to fill the Grand Canyon.

So the more complex the mammal, the stronger the energy, the more the Rotmirage ate.

According to Enzo, the farmers of that land were not good people. They never had been. Enzo knew for a fact that they had a history of incestuous relationships in their family tree and multiple accounts of family members practicing the black arts.

"They picked up Enzo when he was chasing after a mouse in their barn. Otto Clare's son grabbed him by his tail and yanked him into his arms. Before he knew what was happen-

ing, he was in a rusted old cage in the house. There were a lot of cages and various animals in them, all in various stages of emaciation."

Treacle's eyes displayed the sadness and terror that his friend Enzo experienced while on the Clare farm.

It was only blind luck that his cage got kicked and the latch unhinged.

Enzo said he could still hear the crying and wailing of the other animals as they cheered and encouraged him to run. There was nothing he could do for them. He couldn't open their cages, or else he would have. But instead, he slunk around the house, finding an open window that he jumped from, and ran off the property, never looking back.

But before that, Enzo witnessed the Clares' daily rituals, which included summoning the Rotmirage.

They walked about the property with starving animals all around them, without the slightest acknowledgement they were there. It was as if they were just ghastly lawn sculptures or bits of furniture that were only noticed when they were no longer useful.

"How did they summon the Rotmirage? Was it always there, or was it called?"

Enzo said that the monster seemed to appear

whenever Otto Clare wanted. It drained the life out of the animals a little at a time. But the Clares would lure humans there every so often under the guise of land for sale or handyman jobs or even houses for rent. They'd get them to come down County Line Road 63 and lead them into the winding roads, where the Rotmirage would get them lost or confused or tired. The next thing they knew, they'd be at Suicide Bridge. Then life would be too much to bear. Finding a way out would seem impossible. There was no hope anymore.

All of it looked conveniently like a suicide. But it wasn't.

Treacle went on to say that as Enzo got farther away from the house, he thought he'd feel safer, but that wasn't the case. He came to the old bridge and saw a man hanging from his neck. The Rotmirage was hobbling toward the body, giggling and rubbing its twisted and deformed hands together.

"Whatever it was going to do, Enzo didn't know. He was too afraid and ran in another direction, finding his way to the main road and slinking stealthily back to the safety and familiarity of Wonder Falls alleys and streets."

"Were any of the Clares around when Enzo saw the man at Suicide Bridge?" I had to ask.

"No. They were probably conducting their business from the old farmhouse. Enzo said they had several men who visited the farm for a short spell and then left. But they'd return in a week, maybe two, maybe a month."

"Did Enzo see them use any kind of book? Something with spells that can be destroyed?"

"Not that he ever saw. But he said it would be hard to find anything in the main house where they kept him and some other animals. The place was a mess of garbage. They didn't tend to their housekeeping, nor did they mind the acres of farming land they had. It was all just going to waste. It was almost as if they didn't want any life there, nothing growing or producing. But they lorded over every inch of the place like kings. Enzo said they were trapped there but that they liked it."

I shivered.

"You took a big chance coming to the vet's office like that. What if the Rotmirage had gotten you and started sucking your life right out of you? What would I do without you?"

Treacle's pink tongue swept over his whiskers again, and his eyes looked directly into mine.

I know there are "dog people" and "cat people." Don't get me wrong—I love animals, and it's just that plain and simple. But when a cat looks at you like Treacle was looking at me after such an upsetting ordeal, I could see the trust and the love there. He was a good cat, and I'd risk my life for him the same as I would for Bea or Aunt Astrid.

I nodded, but the motion made me cringe.

"Head still hurt?"

"I don't know how Aunt Astrid does it. Passing through doors or walls into other dimensions and back again. I feel like someone bashed me on the head with a brick."

"I'm pretty tired, too."

"Some rest is what we need. Then we have to figure out what to do next. I have a feeling the Clares aren't going to stop, and there will be future generations of them. That is if they can find any women who would want to be part of all that."

Treacle jumped off the counter and walked quietly with me to the bedroom, where he hopped up on the bed and waited as I put on pajamas. I almost skipped the whole evening ritual since pulling my shirt over my head hurt so badly.

Finally, I slowly laid my head down on the pillow, which was normally soft and welcoming but this time felt as if it were made of marble. Treacle encircled my head with his body. The warmth and his gentle purring were like a scalp massage. We were both asleep within minutes. But if it weren't for

Aunt Astrid suffering a little insomnia while keeping an eye on Bea's house and mine, none of us would have known that a large, familiar truck covered in mud drove down our street four times throughout the course of the night.

Help

As if the universe had heard my subconscious plea, the Brew-Ha-Ha did not have its normal line of customers waiting for us to open and pour their steaming cups of coffee. There were a few regulars, but they were low-maintenance patrons, and we loved them for that. Especially today.

"I don't ever want to do that again." Bea looked up to the ceiling and fanned herself with her hand. "I'm breaking out in a cold sweat just thinking about it. There is a reason people are not supposed to pass through walls. My bathroom was the vomitorium last night."

"How are you feeling now?" I asked. My headache was still trying to cling to my brain, with a little ringing in my ears and tingling at the back of my skull, but I could function. In fact, I was looking forward to getting to work and telling my family what Treacle had found out. The big black cat had left early that morning when I opened the kitchen window for a little fresh air. Soon, it would be too cold to let him out all day. He'd have to spend time at the café, as he did every winter around that "*most wonderful time of the year.*" But it was still fall and only a little cold. I didn't have to worry about him. I knew after last night he'd be staying close to home.

"I actually feel really good. So long as I keep the idea of sauerkraut or rice pudding out of my mind." Bea put her hand to her stomach. "I should be fine."

"Sauerkraut. Rice pudding. Got it." I looked at my aunt, who was smiling proudly. "It was just another walk in the park for you," I snapped, unable to control my sarcasm, and that seemed to make Aunt Astrid chuckle even more.

"You girls did great last night, and I know the side effects of passing through solid matter can be debilitating at first, but there is a pleasant side effect that you may not have realized."

I raised my eyebrows at Bea.

"You both admitted to feeling pretty good. Well, lots of bad stuff stays behind on the solid matter as you pass through. Things like caffeine, fluoride, E-coli, tapeworms, and eyelash mites."

"Add eyelash mites to the list of things not to say or think of." Bea grimaced and rubbed her stomach again.

"If you think about it, you both experienced the benefits of an expensive spa treatment without having to spend a nickel." Aunt Astrid put her hands on her hips and smiled. Then she scooted behind the counter and began to slice a big chunk of cherry pie.

"Who is that for?" I murmured.

"It's for Tom," she muttered without turning around. Before I could ask any other questions, the bells over the door jingled, and in stepped a very handsome, very tired-looking Tom Warner. He smiled as he stepped right up to me, kissing me on the cheek. Like the cool cucumber I always am, I blushed and looked down at the floor.

"Hey, Bea. Aunt Astrid," he said before raising his fist to his mouth and stifling a yawn. "You wouldn't happen to have some coffee back there, would you?"

"Especially for you, Tom." Bea turned and grabbed a large cup and filled it to the brim. "Just black, if I remember right?"

"That'll work."

"What's up? Late night?" I asked, patting his shoulder.

"Yeah. I was going to see if you wanted to catch a movie tonight or something, but Officer Brookes is having emergency surgery."

"Oh dear. Is he a friend of yours? Will he be all right?" Aunt Astrid asked as she turned around with the pie in a to-go container and handed it to Tom.

"Yeah. Kidney stones. He was told a couple months ago to go in, but you know how some men can be. Stubborn. So now he's paying the price. But they said he'd pull through just fine. He'll need a little time off is all." Tom looked down at the pie and smiled. "This will be my treat before bed. Thanks, Astrid."

My aunt nodded and turned, grabbing a stack of receipts and taking her place at her favorite small table for two next to the counter to begin counting.

"So I might be out of commission for a week or two. You'll be working when I'm coming home, and I'll be working when you're getting ready to go to sleep."

I tried to pretend that it didn't make any difference to me, but I'm a terrible actress.

"You can always come for your morning coffee. At

least then I'll know you made it through your shift."
I straightened the collar of his uniform shirt.

"I was hoping you'd say something like that." He
squeezed me tightly around the waist, making me
giggle. It was a really gross display. My otherwise
tough-girl persona was completely ruined. Again,
Tom stifled a yawn and took a sip of the coffee. "I
better get going. I'll stop by tomorrow morning."

"Okay." I smiled, letting him kiss me again on the
cheek and leaning into him a little as I felt his strong
arm completely encircle my waist. When he left, I
felt a little strut in my step and wiggled my hips at
my aunt and Bea, who I could feel were staring
at me.

"That poor boy," Aunt Astrid teased as Bea
nodded and went to stand next to her mother.

"Well, as much as I'd like to listen to you two go
on and on about my love life, I am afraid we've got to
focus on something not so comical." I let out a deep
sigh. "Treacle had some information for me last
night." Bea put her hand on her mother's shoulder,
and they both looked at me as though they were
waiting for a bad diagnosis. "We're dealing with
some really sick stuff."

I went on to tell them what Treacle had told me.
When I got to the part about Enzo escaping, I

thought I was going to start crying. This was not the time for mushy sentiment. As much as I hated to do it, I needed to thicken my skin and do it rather quickly, too, because I could feel in my gut what my family was going to say.

"We need to get out there." Aunt Astrid clenched her teeth. "We need to get an idea what the whole place looks like and find the heart of the place. Then we need to stop it from beating."

"I like the sound of that." I rubbed my hands together.

"But, Cath, before you go anywhere, we need to cover up your scent." My aunt stood from her seat and looked seriously at me. I lifted my arm and sniffed.

"Do I offend?"

"Not us. But the Rotmirage knows you." She squinted as if she were playing a life-or-death game of poker. "If it tracked you to the vet's office, it must be looking for you."

"I *don't* like the sound of that." I swallowed hard.

"Mom, I should do this one on my own. Cath shouldn't go. It's too dangerous."

"Hold on," I said. "It's too dangerous for *anyone* to go to that tainted piece of land, but there's no way you're going by yourself."

"Cath has to go," Aunt Astrid solemnly replied. "There will no doubt be animals there, and she'll need to communicate with them. If you don't have that, you'll just be wandering around. I'll be here, managing your protection spell as well as Cath's smell."

"Nice." I rolled my eyes.

"But remember, girls, this is just to collect information. My visions are telling me that we may need to pull out all the stops in order to end this. The Clare roots run very, very deep."

It started to sprinkle rain when Bea and I finally headed out toward County Line Road 63, and my windshield wipers were as old as my car. We were a moving violation of some kind, I was sure of it, but there was no time to waste.

"Wow. You really smell." Bea inhaled deeply. "I think you should let Mom do this again for your next date with Tom. It's intoxicating."

"Oh, ha, ha." I gripped the steering wheel. "Funny, because I can't smell it. What do I smell like?"

"Like a cross between basil and lavender."

"Yikes, you're right." I smiled. "That sounds absolutely wonderful."

"So what is our plan?" Bea looked straight ahead.

"I thought you had something in mind. What are you asking *me* for?" I smirked.

"That sounds about right." Bea smiled and took a deep breath.

We drove around past the spot where Tom had parked the truck when we made our way to Suicide Bridge. We also scooted past the road that led to Archie Jones's home.

"There." Bea pointed to something that was a road in the most basic sense of the word. There was a dusting of gravel that blended into a dirt path wide enough for a small car like mine to maneuver down. I turned and instantly felt a weight fall over the car.

"It's darker in here," Bea whispered, as if something might be listening.

"In more ways than one," I added. The trees bowed close to each other, weaving their branches together in an arch overhead as if they were working together to block out the light. The foliage was thick with wild brambles that were leggy and sprawling around the bases of the trees. "Without a machete or a flame thrower, we aren't going to have a chance of sneaking up on anyone at this point. We'll never get through all that overgrowth."

We drove slowly forward and found a small patch that would camouflage my car if I could carefully ease into it. On my left was a ditch about four feet deep. On my right was a patch of sticker bushes with needles over an inch long.

"This is good," I said. "I think we'll be safe here."

"Safe if we just stayed in the car. But we have to go out there." She pointed a delicate finger ahead into the forest. I could see it tremble slightly.

"Well. It's now or never." We both took a deep breath and quietly opened the car doors, careful not to let the rusty hinges squeak too much, and neither of us slammed them closed.

I listened carefully and could hear the sounds of nature. There weren't many, but they were there. The agitated squawk of a blue jay. The mad rustle of squirrels. But there was nothing else. No sound of traffic in the distance or a random lawnmower getting one last mowing done before the really cold weather came.

Bea's eyes were narrow as she scanned the terrain.

"I get the feeling we should go that way." She pointed to what looked like the entrance of a cave until I squinted. It was a massive tunnel of trees clustered unhealthily together, choking each other out, as some were dying of disease and lack of light, while others grew in twisted, unnatural angles.

Without a word, I nodded. Each step along the sad dirt path sounded like an army of soldiers marching along against the backdrop of a church-quiet forest. Time became abstract, as I thought we had been walking for hours, but we were only on the road for twenty-five minutes. Bea felt the opposite, that we'd only walked for five minutes and had already covered an unnaturally long piece of territory.

"Anyone around that you can ask for directions?" She looked at me and pointed at the ground randomly.

I called out telepathically, as if I were calling for a child in kindergarten or first grade to answer me. The words had to be simple and calm, or else they'd just stare at me or run away. Surprisingly, an answer came from high, high up in a majestic oak tree.

"*You aren't from the bad place.*" It was a hawk. It looked down at us over its proud, robust breast and shifted its strong wings, reminding me of the way James Cagney would adjust his jacket when he played a gangster in the movie *The Roaring Twenties*.

"*No. We're not. But we're trying to find it. Can you tell us where it is?*"

The resplendent creature tilted its head one way and then another as it studied us.

"You mean you can't feel it?"

I held my breath and took an internal inventory of my senses. I was too scared to feel anything else. I shook my head.

The hawk said nothing else telepathically but let out a scratchy cry and dove from the branch it had been perched on. We both watched with wide eyes as it spread its wings and, without flapping them, glided up through the branches and dry leaves without a sound. It headed west, and so did the dirt road that had become little more than a path. So we went west, too.

There were a few pesky flies that circled our heads before being swatted away. Bea had stumbled slightly when her foot caught on a tree root that had surfaced some time ago. I was listening and shivering as the sweat was freezing under my arms and down the spine of my back.

"What is that?" I pointed forward.

At first I thought maybe we had stumbled onto one of those small complexes run by the electric or gas companies where they run services to some of the more rural houses. It was a flat-topped, sprawling structure that had plywood for several windows, and the southeastern edge that we were looking at had burn marks from a fire that had never been repaired. The black burn marks made it look as if there were jagged teeth, and a window devoid of plywood looked like a black, lifeless eye.

There was a faded red barn off behind the building that was closed up tight. Behind that looked like hundreds of shucked rows of corn that hadn't been replanted for at least one farming season.

"Do you think they live there?" Bea asked.

"I don't see anyplace else. My gosh. What a pitiful place to…"

I know Bea didn't hear what I had heard. She couldn't have. She didn't have the gift to speak to animals. But she did have the ability to sense emotions. I heard their cries, but Bea felt their pain and fear.

"There are two of them," I muttered. "And they are in that building."

"Cath, I know what you're thinking, but maybe we should do what Mom said. We know how to get here now. We can come back and pool all our strength. Then we can have a better chance at saving them."

My eyes stung with tears. They were crying, and they were just little kittens.

"I can't leave them, Bea." I wiped my eyes, feeling anger take the place of my fear. "I know what your mom said. But I just can't leave them. They are terrified. It's like leaving crying babies. Neither of us would do that, either."

"No. We wouldn't." Bea squared her shoulders.

There was no need for us to tell each other what we were going to do. It was as if we shared the same brain at times.

Inching our way closer to the edge of the forest where it cleared around the property, we hunched down and watched. There was no movement. Nothing was alive on the outside of the building except the dandelion weeds and crabgrass. A cold wind was whipping up the dead leaves above us.

"Is that the driveway?" I asked, pointing to what looked like a gravel track leading into the woods.

"It looks like it might be. I don't see anything else that looks like a way to get in and out of this place. Other than the path we took." Once again sharing our brain, we both looked behind us as if we had forgotten there might be an angry member of the Clare clan who was sneaking up on us or a Rotmirage out for its daily stroll. All we saw were dry, gray trees and sticker bushes.

"I don't see their truck. At least one of them is gone," I added.

"Maybe both of them." Bea was hoping I'd agree, but I clicked my tongue.

"Maybe there are more of them inside. You know, like when you poke an anthill. Only when they think there is trouble do they all swarm out."

"What a pleasant thought." Bea wrinkled her nose.

"I'm sorry." I rubbed my chin. "I don't know what's wrong with me."

The kittens' cries were becoming louder, so I called out to them. Like human children, it sometimes takes a little finesse to get them to calm down. These little ones were no different.

"Can you hear me?" I called in my mind.

Suddenly, they both became silent.

"I'm here to help. My name is Cath. I can hear you fine if you can just say hello."

Still nothing.

"I am not far away," I said coaxingly. *"Can you tell me anything about where you are?"*

"It's a trick. The bad thing will come again and make us sick," one childlike voice said.

"This doesn't sound like that bad thing," the other kitten replied.

"No. I'm not the bad thing. I am here to take you away

from it. To take you some place safe. Can you tell me where you are?"

That was when I heard the saddest sound that ever hit my ears. Somewhere not far from us, there was a small set of paws frantically clawing at a cage.

"You hear that?" I asked Bea, who nodded. "It's coming from that part of the house. The burnt part."

I took a deep breath and focused.

"I'll go myself."

"Cath, that's too dangerous."

"If anything happens to me, you can get help. There is no need for both of us to go." I was still hunched over as I started to take a couple steps toward the structure in the direction of what looked like a gaping maw.

The sound of the kittens crying was louder still, and I was sure they were there. Without incident, I made it to the building and peeked inside the black eye that was a window.

There, in the middle of a burnt-out kitchen, on two folding chairs, were the cages, which held a kitten each. One was the spitting image of Treacle when he was a baby, except this one had gold eyes. They both looked at me, and I could see they hadn't been fed.

Without a word, I looked around and saw an old

wood crate about six paces away. Without fear, I marched up, grabbed it, and propped it next to the glassless window.

Hoisting myself, I managed to get my stomach over the sill and pull myself inside. It smelled of mold and smoke. With trembling hands, I went to the first cage and slid the lock open. The tabby inside barely put up a fuss. I reached into get her and could feel her ribs against the palm of my hand.

"I'm here to help you." The little creature looked up at me and meowed.

I went to the other cage. Much like Treacle again, this little black fellow was ready for a fight. His tiny needlelike claws came out, and he hissed as he swiped his thin little paw at me. He gouged me good, but I had been gouged by a cat more than once. I bit my tongue, and before he could get me again, I had him in my hand. He was even thinner than the other one.

"Shhh." I nuzzled them against my cheeks. *"Let's get out of here."*

As I turned to climb back out the window, I nearly screamed as I saw a face there.

"Bea? I told you to wait."

"A truck just pulled up."

My eyes widened, and the kittens began to whimper.

"Here. Take them." I handed the kittens to Bea through the window. She took the little creatures, and I knew instantly she would bring them comfort with her touch. She stuffed them inside her shirt and cradled them with her arms.

At the other end of the bunker, I heard a door open. Looking around, I saw a strange ladder that led up to what must have been an attic at one time. Without giving Bea a chance to say anything, I dashed up the rickety old ladder, hoping it wouldn't wait until I was at the very top to give way.

"Cath!" Bea hissed.

"Get help," I mouthed then disappeared into the blackened ceiling.

Not the First

꧁꧂

No sooner had I pulled my feet up into the black darkness of the attic than I heard the *clump-clump-clump* of heavy work boots on the floor. Whoever it was stomped through the house but didn't make his way to the kitchen.

I pulled myself into a small dark corner, tucking my legs underneath me while I squinted, letting my eyes get used to the darkness.

There was very little space for me to stand up. The highest height I could reach was on my knees with my back hunched over. There were small pockets of light where the floor of the attic had broken. They looked like small suns in the vast blackness but gave me enough light to see that I could, if I were careful, inch my way from one end of the complex to the other. It was one long space between the ceiling of the rooms below and the roof above my head.

Two long beams ran the length of the place. They were about the width of railroad ties but not nearly as thick or sturdy. Moving in slow motion, I placed one hand on the beam and tested its strength. It seemed solid enough at this point, so I carefully leaned all my weight on it before swinging my knee on board. Holding my breath, I listened for any groans or snaps from the wood, indicating it wasn't going to hold me up. There was nothing.

So, with cold sweat still rolling down the center of my back and under my arms, now spreading to my forehead, I inched my way to an opening in what was my floor but the Clares' ceiling.

What I saw below was disgusting. It was as if they lived in a shanty. There were sleeping bags on the floor. More than two, so I wasn't sure how many people actually lived here, but suddenly, I was afraid for Bea, who was hopefully making her way back to the car without anyone noticing her.

Dishes crusted over with barnacles of dried food

were also on the floor and stacked on TV trays. Melted candles of various colors and sizes were standing in plates and on the wooden floor itself. But the most disturbing thing was the symbols and letters spray-painted on the walls and floor.

We weren't just looking at a pentagram that some high school kid scribbled out in an attempt to be edgy and gothic. This was a mega-pentagram with symbols and notations only someone like Aunt Astrid would know. The only reason I recognized it was because I had seen it in one of my aunt's books. One that was written in a language I couldn't read with instructions I couldn't follow and pictures I couldn't even look at without getting the heebie-jeebies.

This was hardcore black magic. Chaos magic.

"Where's the water?" The heavy-sounding voice startled me out of my thoughts, and I was sure I gasped so loud they heard me. I don't know how long I held my breath and listened. If the Clares had heard me, they didn't let on.

"Where's the water?" he said again. It was Otto Clare, the older man. He was the one stomping around.

"It's in the pitcher," the younger Clare said. He

walked past the hole in the ceiling but didn't look up. He had a tattoo snaking its way up the back of his neck. I could see from the T-shirt he was wearing that his muscular arms were also covered in ink. Designs of devils and monsters and flames writhed every time his muscles flexed.

I wondered why he wasn't cold. The temperature had dropped, and even though it should be hotter in the darkness of the attic, I was freezing.

Otto Clare walked somewhere else in the room, and I heard him pick something up. A second later, the sound of water splattering on the floor came up to me. I wondered if he had drunk some or poured it on his head or chest or just dumped it on the floor. Truthfully, I thought that was probably how they bathed. Looking at what they lived in, I would guess Civil War–era soldiers in the field had better hygiene.

Another car was approaching. From the direction of the long gravel trail Bea and I had seen, I could hear a car with a souped-up exhaust system that made it grumble at stoplights and roar through yellow lights, making a person's chest vibrate deep inside.

"He's early," Otto Clare said to his younger, tattooed offspring. "Go tell him to wait."

Early? I wondered. Early for what? What were they doing?

It didn't take long for me to talk myself into inching a little deeper inside the house. I wanted to see who was driving that noisy car. What was he there for, and what did he want with the Clares?

There was no mention of Bea, and so far, I was sure they hadn't noticed the kittens were missing. While I was up in the attic, I heard a scurrying to my left. The corners in between the rafters and along the floor were blacker than black. Squinting didn't do me any good, so I gave a telepathic shout.

"Hey little one! Can you hear me?"

"Yes."

"Can you tell me what's going on down there?"

The tiniest mouse appeared as just a fuzzy ball not far from my hand. I could see his silhouette against the fingers of light that reached delicately into the attic.

"Men in and out. Growing sad plants."

"Are there any other animals in cages or hiding like you?"

"All dead. You can't hide like me. You'll be dead, too."

"What do you mean?"

"Anything that's living gets eaten from the inside out."

"By what?"

"*Sometimes by themselves. Sometimes by the other thing.*"

The front door slammed, and the tattooed Clare came stomping in with another man behind him. The mouse quickly jumped back into the shadows and disappeared. I gripped the beam I was on and listened.

"You're early. It's not ready," Otto Clare grumbled.

"Well, let's hurry it up. It's bad enough I have to drive all the way out here twice a month."

Otto Clare didn't answer, and I couldn't see exactly what was happening. But the man's response gave me a pretty clear indication.

"Okay. Take your time. I'm not in any real hurry. I'll wait outside."

The door slammed again.

I heard Otto Clare walking to another room and followed him as best I could. A quarter-sized hole in the floor shined up at me. I leaned down and saw what the man was there to get.

Sitting on an old bureau was a scale, some plates, several bags of different-colored pills, white powder, and a plastic trashcan filled to the top with marijuana.

After all this, these guys are drug dealers? I was

fascinated and terrified all at once. With slow, deliberate movements, Otto Clare measured out pills and powder and strong-smelling buds of the dried plant and put them in separate bags. I started to wonder how everything fit together.

Archie Jones started it all with his suicide. But Jake did say they found traces of horse tranquilizers in his system. I bet, if tested, some of that powder would turn out to be that stuff. If Archie stumbled across this place, that would have been all the reason they needed to make sure he didn't talk.

But what about the Rotmirage? Where did that thing fit in?

Suddenly, the tattooed Clare walked in and stood next to his father.

"Do you smell that?"

I froze. I had forgotten all about Aunt Astrid's smell spell. Here I was, as fragrant as a rose in early morning, plopped in the middle of a burnt-out domicile that reeked of smoke and rot.

"What?"

Tattooed Clare sniffed the air.

"Smells like a funeral parlor."

Ouch! Unnecessary. Really.

However much that comment might have hurt my feelings, it meant something more to Otto Clare.

He stopped what he was doing and looked at his son. Then he sniffed the air. I couldn't see his face and didn't dare lean down any further. But I could see his hands flying back and forth over the bureau, and they started to tremble.

"That's not a good sign."

"What should we do?"

"Give Rank his stuff. Get our money. We'll deal with it once he's gone."

The sound of boots and a slamming screen door had become familiar. I needed to look in the other rooms, but in order to do that, I would have to find my way across some of the insulation. There was no telling how weak or rotten the wood had become. Not to mention spiders. So far I had been able to push the fact out of focus that they probably surrounded me and that at any second one might just crawl in my hair. But if I was going to do this, I was going to have to face my fear—arachnophobia.

Again, I focused on the situation at hand. Was I really going to be scared of these eight-legged creatures when there were literal murdering drug dealers just a few feet from me? I was trespassing on their property. Technically, they had the right to kill me. Plus, I'd seen the drugs. I knew what they were doing. Was a spider really scarier? That depended on the size. Everyone knew that.

I took a deep breath and held it. With bravery I was scraping up from the soles of my feet, I carefully turned myself toward what would be the back of the house and to the left of the gravel driveway that was outside. There was a hole the size of my fist that was between the support beam I had been utilizing this whole time and a smaller beam that showed through worn-out layers of insulation. I stretched a trembling hand out and felt the wood, pushing on it slightly to see if there was any cracking sound or rotten feeling to it. All I felt were the petrified remains of what that mouse left behind and a layer of dust so thick my hands were sure to be nearly black with filth.

Contorting my body as though I were playing a game of Twister, I leaned over the hole and carefully looked in. I gasped. The walls were covered in more spray paint. This time, it was the image of the Rotmirage that stared back at me. Even in plain black paint against what had once been a room with white walls and a wooden floor, the image was terri-fying. The blank, two-dimensional eyes stared at me from the wall. Without realizing it, I leaned back out of its view just in case. Mystic symbols that should never see the light of day were broadcast across the walls and floor.

In the middle of the room, stuffed into several large garbage bags, was money. If I had to guess, I would have said there was over a million dollars in cash just sitting there in the middle of this broken-down room, with nothing but a painted image of the Rotmirage to watch over it.

The rumble of the car the dude named Rank drove started up again. With all that noise to cover my movements, I shifted my body and maneuvered my way to a second, larger hole that was about the size of my head. I was about to peek down when I heard Otto Clare start to yell.

"Leland!" he screamed. His voice shook the whole place. Within seconds, the rumbling engine began to recede as it obviously drove back down the gravel road it originally travelled. "Leland! They're gone!"

The thought hit me across the chest, knocking out my breath. He was talking about the kittens. But how had he gotten to that room without my hearing him? I didn't hear Otto Clare take a single step. Yet his voice was coming from that part of the complex. Quickly, I scurried to what seemed to be the darkest corner of the attic. I flattened myself down between the support beam and a reinforcement beam, pulling a small tuft of insulation up for additional camouflage.

The idea of one of the Clares making his way up that old ladder, this head swiveling from side to side as he scanned the attic for signs of an intruder, terrified me. Drug dealers were known to kill without mercy. Demonic, Rotmirage-worshipping drug dealers were probably a tad worse.

Leland came running back in from outside. I heard his heavy boots and the screen door slam.

"You didn't lock the cages," the old man hissed.

"I did. You were right here when I did it."

"Well, obviously, you didn't do it right. It isn't like when we had the horses. It could use those for months."

Someone shuffled their feet and paced nervously.

"I'll go out and get another one. There are plenty of alley cats. Stray dogs. I could even steal one from a fenced-in yard if I have to," Leland muttered.

Hearing him say he'd just collect some stray cats made my blood boil but filled me with sadness. Of course, I thought of my Treacle. Those poor kittens we had taken out of here. How many more had died in the meantime, before Tamara had her terrifying experience and Archie Jones was murdered? That was probably where the soul parasites came from. Aunt Astrid had said they thrived in massive graves. With all these acres of land, the Clares could have dumped the bodies anywhere or everywhere.

"And your bones might join them." Was that my thought or something else in my head? I peeked up, but still no one was looking at me from the steps. Looking to my right, I saw no grotesque, milky eyes staring at me from a head that was up through one of the many holes. I was alone.

I began to wonder what time it was. It had to be getting darker outside. Did Bea make it back to the car, or did the woods turn her around so she was still out there wandering and looking for the car? Did she still have the kittens, or did they scratch their way away from her, trust in humans completely shattered and gone?

And if Bea hadn't gotten away, if she didn't go to get help, how long would I last up here before they would find me? How long was I going to be able to stay hidden? Would I ever see Tom again? Would I ever see Blake again?

Now why in the world would I be thinking about him at a time like this? It was ridiculous. Some might say it bordered on a sickness or something. Tom was the one who was handsome and funny and bought wonderful presents and, most importantly, understood what I was. What I am. And I wanted to see him again.

"There ain't no time for all that. Tomorrow, you'll get me some replacements. But tonight, you know what needs to be done." Otto Clare's voice sounded almost relieved at whatever cryptic message he was conveying.

"No, Dad. I can get another animal. It won't take me any time at all. Just don't call it yet and..."

"Don't call it?" Otto Clare laughed sadistically. "Let you get away with neglecting your duties? Now, son, you know I can't do that. Look what happened to your older brother when I let him off the hook. You want to take that risk?"

Leland didn't make a sound.

"You remember what he looked like after that? We had to keep him chained up in the barn until the whole thing was over. Buried him next to your mom in the family plot. You remember?"

"Dad, let me go get another one. Please."

This wasn't just a family drug business. There was something frightfully oppressive working on this family. I had to get out of here. I had to get back to Bea and Aunt Astrid and Tom and tell them they needed to sweep this whole area. There were bodies here, and I'd bet my last dollar there was more than one restless soul among them. But all I could do now was wait.

"Sorry, son. Sometimes we have to learn the hard way." Otto Clare began to mumble something. His voice moved from the back of the house to the front, almost directly beneath me. Leland's footsteps followed. Funny how again I didn't hear the old man's footsteps. That was just plain weird.

Otto Clare's voice wove together a string of words that to the untrained ear sounded like mad babblings. A person with Tourette syndrome might sound like this.

But I knew what he was doing. I had seen my aunt slip into spell-recitation mode a hundred times. He was calling something. I knew what that was, too.

Slowly, I crawled out from my hiding place and tenderly inched my way to the room I thought the Clares were in. They were in what was the front room by the door.

Otto Clare's voice was low and scratchy and menacing. His son paced back and forth nervously. It was as if he was waiting for his father to stop what he was doing and show some compassion. But it didn't happen.

I couldn't imagine what Leland was thinking. My own mother dove right into the path of a monster to save me. Here Otto Clare was, practically feeding his son to one. I was witnessing abuse, and no matter how big and scary Leland Clare was, he was still this man's son. My heart ached a little for him.

But quickly enough, I heard that sound. That familiar sound that made my skin itch to tear itself from my bones and get away. The sound that made my heart thud in my chest even though all my insides felt as if they had sunk to my feet. The sweat on my body became a sheet of ice.

"*Let me in,*" it cried in that singsongy voice. "*Let me in.*"

With more stealth than I knew I was capable of, I shifted over and balanced on two beams so I could look outside in the direction I thought the Rotmirage was coming from. Once again, its body was all hunched over as it dug at the foundation of the building. Why did it do that? Why didn't it just climb through the open window, as I did? What was the purpose of burrowing and clawing at the foundation?

As it scratched at the ground, it kicked the dirt up behind it, as a dog might. It was feverishly digging and making horrible grunting noises before it would stop and move a few feet farther down the base of the house and start again. In between, it would sing, *"Let me in, let me in."*

Finally, it slipped out of view, and I went back to where the Clares were waiting. But when I looked down the hole, I saw them standing there. Otto Clare was all swollen up with contempt as he stared at his son. Leland looked past his father toward the door, ready to take his punishment.

The Rotmirage suddenly appeared. First it was a gnarly arm that shot straight up through the floor. Except it wasn't the actual floor. It pushed its way through the delicate membrane that separated this dimension from another one. That would explain why there was dead silence when Bea and I had gone to explore County Line Road 63. My gosh. What was all this?

The hideous creature strained and struggled as it pulled itself up. The boney hoof clomped on the floor, but I really couldn't tell if that was a real sound or just in my head. What I was seeing, I was sure no one was supposed to see. When Aunt Astrid slipped into other dimensions, it was seamless, and she disturbed nothing. The Rotmirage treated the delicate layers as it did the rough ground outside. It tore through them, ripping and scratching away at the astral fiber like a child ripping open a present. There was no regard for the order of things.

When it finally emerged, it rose from its twisted and hunched position and towered over Otto Clare, who barely showed any sign of fear, if you didn't notice the trickle of sweat down the side of his forehead.

Leland, on the other hand, visibly shook yet stood still and stared at the Rotmirage, which was heaving and puffing as it stared at him.

It had to be Aunt Astrid's spell that had me veiled from this thing. It wouldn't have missed me had I not had the universe working to conceal me from this evil.

The Rotmirage growled. The singsongy, innocent, and childlike voice had contorted into a gravelly, animalistic snarl completely devoid of compassion. Long, black, needlelike nails grew from its twisted and knotty fingers. As I looked at them, they wavered like heat rising off the pavement in the summertime. Were they real? As real in this world as the Rotmirage was, I suppose.

The right hand snapped to Leland's head, and the left went to his side. I blinked, and those horrific hands were positioned on the young man's person. He didn't say a word. He didn't cry out or scream.

But I watched as his eyes reddened and filled with tears. If this was what it did to this strong young man, what chance did an animal in a cage or stall have? My own eyes stung with tears.

The Rotmirage arched its back, and its mouth stretched open and shut in a grotesque manner, like someone no longer in charge of their faculties trying to express that they need help. Its black tongue rolled out sloppily.

Leland's body began to shake. He was becoming smaller. His muscular shoulders deflated, and his chest caved in. Within seconds, it was a full-on seizure.

"You stop that now!" Otto Clare shouted with his lips pulled back from his teeth in an intolerant sneer. "You take your licks! You brought this on yourself!"

But Leland didn't hear him. He had slipped away to a place that was pitch darkness, and I think he preferred that. It was like sleep, except when he woke up, there was a good chance he might not remember everything that happened. He might have the worst of it wiped from his memory. He'd forget how long it lasted. He might also forget what he saw as it happened. But the one thing he wouldn't forget was that his father allowed it.

"It's what needs to be done! You're not the first—

you just remember that!" Otto Clare yelled at his son then turned and walked in his silent manner out of the room.

I did hope Leland was in that dark place. Had my mother walked out of my bedroom instead of standing her ground and telling the beast "NO! You won't hurt my daughter!" I would have died in more ways than one. Leland was dying just a little bit at a time.

I couldn't watch anymore. I bowed my head and squeezed my eyes shut, but then I felt it. As if my nerves were not taxed already, along the back of my neck, I felt it. Eight furry legs that quickly touched down on the exposed skin of my nape and flitted around the circumference of my neck toward my exposed ear.

Now, I know what people might be thinking. Here I am, in the midst of a paranormal torture session, completely unseen and safe for all intents and purposes. But irrational fears have this way of making me act irrational.

Suddenly, I knew the intentions of this eight-legged beast. It had been sizing me up in its cluster of eight eyes, and it thought this was the opportunity of a lifetime. Drop down on a silent web under cover of darkness, make way to inner ear canal, and have babies.

Everything became a blur as I waved my arms in the air then slapped my face, shaking my head and trying to get the thing off my skin without having to actually touch it. I don't remember screaming, but I don't think I was completely silent.

When I held still to see if I felt anything still moving on my face, I just happened to look at the hole in the floor. Except it was no longer a hole. It was the pasty, contemptuous face of the Rotmirage protruding through the attic floor.

This time, I screamed.

Without thinking, I pushed myself back onto the carpet of fiberglass insulation. The wooden frame-work was not nearly as sturdy as the crossbeam down the middle. I felt the plaster starting to give way beneath me. I was backward, with my feet in front of me and my hands behind me, as I stared at the Rotmirage pulling itself up into the attic.

"You're not going anywhere, girl," came the voice of Otto Clare to my right. I looked and saw his head peeking up from the stairs I had climbed up a few hours earlier. Just as I said I *didn't want to see.*

I didn't know where I thought I could go, but I pushed myself back even further into the darkness.

Just as my back was about to hit the wall, I heard another sound. It was like the voice of an angel. A police siren.

Even though Otto Clare's face was in darkness, I could see he no longer felt as confident as he had a second ago. He slithered back down the hole he'd crawled up from and down the steps.

The Rotmirage, on the other hand, wasn't shaken in the least. It licked its lips, a continual hiss coming from its mouth. I turned to try and go down the rotten steps, but my weight was too much for the rotten beams. Before I knew what was happening to me, I landed with a thud on the floor in the room with all the money. Of course, I couldn't have landed on all those soft bags of cash. I had to just miss them and use my right shoulder and knee to soften my fall.

Falling pieces of wood and shredded insulation cascaded down around me. I was sure the head of the Rotmirage would follow soon since I could hear it still hissing and gurgling at my disappearing act. But I wasn't going to wait around for it to start looking for me. Neither was I going to wait for Otto Clare to come get me and have this whole thing develop into some kind of hostage crisis.

Standing up made my entire right side light up

with pain. My shoulder felt as if it had been jammed underneath my neck, and my knee had swollen up underneath my pants. The window was covered with aluminum foil to keep out most of the light. But a slight ribbon of dusk came through. When I ripped the flimsy material away, I was face to face with Bea.

We both screamed.

Some Creatures Have No Decency

Laughing through my terror, I unlocked the rickety window and pushed it up just as thunderous steps were pounding up behind me.

"Otto and Leland Clare! This is the Wonder Falls Police Department!"

I recognized that voice.

"We've got you surrounded! Come out with your hands up!"

Without looking behind me, I heard those big clodhoppers stop in their tracks. Busted shoulder and bum knee or not, I launched myself through that open window with the grace of a gazelle leaping over a smooth pool of water left from the rainy season. Okay, maybe it was more like a turtle sliding off a rock. Either way, I was out of there. Thankfully, Bea broke my fall this time.

"Are you all right?" She squeezed me tightly.

"I'm a little beat up but okay. The kittens?"

"They are safe at Mom's with Marshmallow, Peanut Butter, and Treacle."

"Girls." Aunt Astrid's voice was loud and firm. "We've got some work to do."

What I found out later was that the Rotmirage had once been human, a regular person who found a way to slip in and out of dimensions. What my aunt later explained was that since the Clares came from a long line of black witches, the chances were pretty good this Rotmirage was one of their ancestors. Maybe even the wife of Otto and mother of Leland.

But I didn't know any of this when I stood on my stronger left leg and leaned on Bea for support.

"What do we need to do?" I asked.

"We need to give this creature a proper burial," my aunt said as she stepped up to the window.

"She's not going in there, is she?" I gripped Bea's hand tightly in mine.

"She doesn't have to," Bea said defiantly. "She's going to bring it out here."

It was an extraction spell. Aunt Astrid had used it on me more than once when I was a kid and had a splinter from climbing trees, or the time as an adult when I swallowed a plastic toothpick holding together a turkey sandwich I was having for lunch.

As she began to recite the words, Bea and I joined in for the refrain. The words were old and sounded like crunching hard candy. But it didn't take long before the Rotmirage was reluctantly being pulled from the house.

Once again, not a single fiber of wood or plaster was disturbed. But I heard a tear, like a rag being ripped, as Aunt Astrid reached out her hands to the space in front of her. She was a mime heaving an invisible rope. It didn't take long for a hoof of the Rotmirage to appear from inside the house. Then the second hoof came through.

The red and blue lights of more than one squad car on the other end of the house distracted me. I could hear the voice through the megaphone as the police were trying to get the Clares out of the house. I didn't see any guns when I was in their domicile, but what drug dealer doesn't have guns handy? I've seen enough episodes of *COPS* to know the answer is none.

Aunt Astrid was struggling. Bea stepped closer to her, but I was distracted. My shoulder and knee were throbbing. But that was secondary. There was a man on the other side of this house trying to coax a couple of lunatics outside so they could be arrested. No one ever goes peacefully. These were people who had a relationship with a malevolent entity. If Otto Clare was willing to feed his own son to the Rotmirage, he would have no problem hurting anyone else. Like Archie Jones. Like heaven knows who else.

It wasn't until the whole grotesque Rotmirage poured through its dimension into this one that I realized I was needed right here. It lurched forward and swiped at my aunt, who merely leaned back to avoid its swing.

As I studied her face, I didn't know how she maintained her cool. She looked like someone who had done this a million times before. But before I could warn her, those needlelike nails emerged from its hands, and my aunt didn't escape their scratch.

Three deep slashes appeared across Aunt Astrid's right shoulder, and she shrieked in pain.

"*Mom!*" Bea yelled and let go of my hand in order to support her mother. That was exactly what the Rotmirage wanted. The chain was broken. Our power lessened. It quickly got the upper hand. Before Bea even saw it coming, the creature stretched its twisted arm out like the thick branch of a tree and knocked her almost ten feet back.

My aunt continued to chant, her words rising over the sound of the other approaching sirens and that of the police shouting as something else was happening on the other side of the house and out of view. I took off to help Bea.

"Hey, girl." I slipped my arm underneath her head, and as much as I hate to admit it, I sort of slapped her cheeks. I had to. I needed her to snap out of it and shake the cobwebs from her head so we could get back in the fight. "You've gotten the eight count. Now back on your feet."

"What are you talking about?" She squinted and shook her head.

"That!" I pointed to the Rotmirage.

"For a second, I was hoping it was a dream." She got back to her feet. We had to look like a very imposing pair as I limped with my shoulder slung back and Bea rubbed her jaw and the back of her head. But as we reached Aunt Astrid, the game suddenly changed.

"What's it doing?" Bea asked her mother.

The Rotmirage stepped back on its hooves, partially concealed beneath the white gown it was wearing. At first I thought it was crying, but that wasn't it. It was laughing. The thing was nearly hysterical, and it wasn't a pleasant laugh like the giggle of a baby or when your best friend laughs at a story you tell. It was madness. It poured from the open maw in waves.

The wind picked up and tore through the trees around us. Clouds rolled across the purple-and-blue sky. Aunt Astrid began shouting at the top of her lungs. Bea and I rejoined her, doing our part, determined to bind this thing and send it back to where it came from.

But it wasn't going.

Its white eyes focused on us, it spat at us. Literally. Gross, I know.

"We must be getting to it," I yelled to Bea. Even though she was right next to me, the wind was taking away the sounds. It was strange with all the commotion how clearly I could hear everything. That was when I felt the pit of my stomach collapse. It wasn't just going to leave and go back to its dimension. It was going to take us with it. Somehow, it had us trapped with it in this alternative dimensional bubble, and if it went, we went with it.

"Stop!" I cried. "Aunt Astrid, stop the chant!"

"No, Cath!" Bea stared at me. "We can't stop now!"

"But don't you see? It's going to take us with it! We'll be its prisoners!"

"That is always a chance when you do what we do," Aunt Astrid said calmly. "The three of us are just not enough strength to destroy it. But we can send it back. And we are willing to accept the cost."

Aunt Astrid resumed her incantation as if she had done nothing more than tell me the time. Then I thought about my mother. She had done the same thing. She had sacrificed her life for me. She didn't even think twice—she just did it.

I'd really like to be able to say that I squared my shoulders, dug in my heels, and joined my aunt and cousin willingly in this ultimate sacrifice. It would be great to say I faced death and smiled. But I'd be lying through my teeth.

"What?" I screamed. "You guys didn't send me that memo!" I did dig in my heels, and I started to shout the refrain to my aunt's spell. I pulled every bit of energy I could muster from everything around me. But I could feel myself slipping. The ground was getting softer. The air was getting heavier. Wherever we were headed, I had a distinct feeling it wasn't going to be pleasant.

Then, suddenly, a charge of energy coursed up my leg from an unlikely source.

"*You!*" I looked down and nearly cried. "You must be Enzo!"

The orange-and-white cat looked up at me.

"I've been waiting for my chance," the little animal said telepathically. With ease and grace, he jumped up onto my shoulder and perched himself there.

Cats are like lightning rods for energy. As soon as he joined us, he more than provided the necessary power we needed.

The hideous contortion on the Rotmirage's face quickly changed from glee to horror. Although neither Bea nor I could see exactly what happened, Aunt Astrid and Enzo could.

"It's got it!" Enzo shouted. *"Its got the thing tied up in its vines!"*

I was glad I couldn't see exactly what was happening. But I did watch as the Rotmirage bucked and swatted and screamed as if a swarm of bees had descended on it.

Something grabbed it around the middle and, folding the Rotmirage in two, pulled it into a hole no bigger than a frying pan. Its shriveled and knotty body creased unnaturally as it was slowly sucked in, and within the blink of an eye, it was gone.

Sound had returned to the clearing. But before we could celebrate, Enzo fell from my shoulder.

"Wait!" I scooped him in my arms. "Good kitty. We'll get you some help." My eyes teared as I looked into his. *"This is Bea. She's my best friend in the whole world. She can help you. I promise."*

"The bad thing is gone now. It won't hurt anyone else. It won't be summoned back."

"No. I promise." I handed him off to Bea, who began to use her magic on him instantly. I scratched his head for a moment to catch my breath and comfort the feline. But then I heard shots fired on the other side of the house.

"Oh no." I looked to my aunt.

"Cath, don't go out there. Just stay here and let the police do what they do. They don't need our help."

"But he's out there," I said, fretting.

"And he knows we're here. Don't be a distraction. Come on. We need to get away from this place until it is settled with the Clares once and for all."

So the three of us Greenstones headed for shelter under the cover of the dark trees. There was a shift in the air, and as scary as the verdure was when Bea and I had snuck up here earlier today, it was serene and almost inviting now.

Bea stroked Enzo's fur, and I could see how she was working her magic on his aura and life force. If he could just hold on, we could take him to Old

Murray Willis, who ran the animal shelter in Wonder Falls.

I studied Bea's face to see if there was any indication as to how good or bad Enzo's condition really was.

"How did you know we were here?" I asked the cat, who had begun to purr and close his eyes.

"I went to visit Treacle. He said he was going to join the other familiars to add their strength to your quest to rid the world of that bad thing. I thought if you were here, there was a chance to get rid of it."

"If it weren't for you we might have failed."

Enzo meowed weakly.

"You rest now," I continued. *"Bea will take care of you."*

Bea's expression had not changed. She was still seeing into Enzo's aura. Her hands waved back and forth as though she were conducting a symphony. She saw everything. All I saw was Enzo finally relaxed. I had no idea the amount of damage that had been done.

"Aunt Astrid, are you okay?" I limped to my aunt's side. She had taken a seat on a log and was catching her breath.

"Yes, honey. I'm fine. That was a rough one." She tenderly poked at her shoulder where the Rotmirage had ripped her blouse. "This was one of my favorite shirts, too. Some creatures have no decency."

I rubbed my shoulder and eased down on the ground. But my insides were not calm. They were jittery, like live electrical wires that have been severed during a storm.

"I can't stand this. I've got to go see what's happening," I said.

"Cath, you're busted up. You can't run. You can't swing your arm to even try and defend yourself. Do you want to get him or one of his men killed because you just wanted to see what was happening?"

Before I could answer that, there was a giant boom, and smoke filled the whole complex. It poured out the window I had raised and billowed out the open end that had been burnt some time ago. The sounds of men rushing in and shots being fired filled the clearing, causing nighttime birds to take flight. Only then did I realize how cold I was, and I began to shake.

Out of the Ordinary

✦❧✦

By the time we heard the house had been cleared and the Clares were in custody, I thought I was going to lose my mind.

"Go ahead, honey," Bea encouraged me. "I'll take care of him." She snuggled Enzo to her. He looked as if he was sleeping contentedly in her arms, and I could hear his motor running softly.

My aunt nodded and waved me on. I shambled around the back of the house toward the red and blue lights that were still sweeping across the property. There were several men in SWAT gear with their faces covered. I looked to the squad cars, hoping I'd see that familiar face behind the wheel, on a cell phone call, or going over the situation with another officer.

When the ambulance arrived, my heart pounded, and I watched as two men jumped out of the back, pulling a stretcher to a man lying on the ground.

I didn't know if I should even go over there. The last time I mixed business with pleasure, it came back to bite me. But I had to know.

"What happened to you?"

The voice I had been waiting to hear startled me.

"Tom?" He was underneath a bulletproof vest, headgear, and a visor and had a rifle in his hands. I fell into his arms and squeezed him tightly. "I was so worried. I heard the gunshots and thought the worst."

"It was a little hairy there for a while, but we managed to make it out okay."

"What about the man on the stretcher? Will he be all right?" I jerked my thumb in the direction of the ambulance.

"Diaz? Yes. He got grazed in the leg. But thankfully, it didn't hit an artery. He'll have a cool scar to show his grandkids."

Tom lifted his visor, and before I could say another word, he kissed me. It felt as if it had been a hundred years since he had done that.

"Are you mad at me?" I blubbered.

"I just kissed you with as much passion as I could

muster with the rest of the troops milling around. What would make you say that?"

"Because I am here. It's my fault, and one of your men got shot because you guys were here to..."

Tom slipped his hand underneath my arm and led me away from the crowd of people. He took off his helmet, and his hair was sweaty and curly and stuck to his head in a really sexy and masculine way. Not that I was looking for that—I'm just telling it as it is.

"Your cousin called me. She told me where you were and what happened. Call it coincidence if you want. I'll call it divine intervention. But my boys were already planning a raid of the Clare property."

I rubbed my aching shoulder and listened.

"I asked Bea if there was anything 'out of the ordinary' I should know about." He used finger quotes for those four little words. "And she said most definitely. So against my better judgment, I told her to hightail it out here and get gone whatever it was that you needed gone. She said something about Rot Gut or..."

"The Rotmirage. That was the thing that you and I saw."

"Just when I had finally started sleeping with the lights off again, that horrible memory has to be brought back." He squeezed me tenderly around the waist. "It was a terrible risk. I knew what kind of people we were dealing with, and I was afraid after I had hung up the phone that I might have just sent your cousin and your sweet aunt to their dooms. Not to mention that when I heard you were stuck here, I was terrified."

"So I'm not in trouble?" I was almost shocked.

"Not with me, you're not."

I know this isn't the time or place to gush on about it, but Tom's dimples were so deep and cute when he smiled that I couldn't resist smiling back. I tried to go up on tiptoes and kiss him again, but the pain in my knee nearly knocked me over.

"You never did tell me. What happened to you?" He held me up with his strong arm.

"I fell through the ceiling," I whined.

"What?"

"Yeah. The Rotmirage had me cornered in the attic. But I got away. I just fell through the ceiling, is all."

"That is *so* cool."

"A spider crawled on me."

Tom looked at me and shivered.

"Was it big?" he asked with eyes wide and serious.

"Felt like a tarantula. It crawled on my neck and cheek."

"My poor baby," he cooed. "That must have been horrible for you."

"It was." I shivered, too.

"I mean, doing battle with interdimensional demons and ruthless drug dealers is a major inconvenience. But a spider on your skin by your face and so close to your hair, well, that's almost too much for any one person to endure."

"You understand me so well."

Tom had another officer take the Clares to the station for booking. But before they were loaded into the squad car, I saw them, sitting with their legs stretched out in front of them to balance while their hands were handcuffed behind them. It was as if I were seeing not them but maybe their twins. They looked the same yet not so much.

Otto Clare was no longer that strong, imposing man that sent fear into the very marrow of my bones. His hair was still there but wispier as the wind pushed it over his scalp. Dark age spots dotted his skin, which was paler now and quite sickly looking as blue and purple veins mapped their way underneath. His clothes had become baggier, as if he had shrunk while wearing them.

Leland Clare was even more transformed. Within the span of seconds, his round, muscular shoulders and broad chest had become edgy, like a Picasso image. Weird angles and strange coloring defined his bones and sinewy muscles, which were defined and defiled by so many horrible tattoos.

The one thing that hadn't changed was the look behind their eyes. They stared at me. I could see the shadow of something sinister behind their eyes, like a chick tussling around inside an egg that had just a small crack in it. The beast couldn't get out, but it was using every bit of energy it had to try.

They hated me. I was going to be blamed for this in their rotted-out brains. They wouldn't forget the name Greenstone, I was sure. But alone, as they were right now, they were finally feeling what it must have been like for all the animals and people that had died on this property. Trapped and scared and hopeless.

I stared back at them. They had no idea what kinds of things I had seen in my life already. The glare of a couple of demon-worshipping drug dealers was hardly enough to make me lose sleep tonight. It crossed my mind to tell them that it was the power of one cat, one that they didn't kill, that caused their bodyguard to be sent back to where it came from, but I didn't. The look and smell of decay and rust was already settling over them, and I'd be surprised if they didn't both end up stark raving mad within the next few days.

The property was roped off with police tape. As the sun started to come up, there were four cadaver dogs searching the property along with helicopters with some fancy capabilities that would indicate if any bodies were buried on the premises.

The weird thing, as if the whole situation wasn't weird enough, was that the mirage that added a piece of property that wasn't really there vanished with the Rotmirage. What the police found in its place was a marijuana crop tucked in behind the forest that surrounded it and the dying crops of corn that surrounded the forest.

"That was how they were making so much money," Tom said two days later when he came into the Brew-Ha-Ha.

"Oh, I saw the bags of money there," I boasted. "Did you see where I fell through the ceiling?" I nodded but stopped as it hurt my shoulder, which was currently in a sling. My knee also had a brace on it. When I walked down the street, I did an excellent imitation of Boris Karloff as *The Mummy*.

"Are you kidding? I told my partner and the

police photographer that that was where my girl-friend fell through the ceiling." He rocked back and forth on his heels. "They were totally amazed and jealous."

I looked at Bea, whose eyes widened, and a smirk fell across her lips. She had suffered a goose egg on the back of her head but other than that was okay. My aunt sat at her favorite table for two with a stack of receipts that she was reconciling as she listened. I saw the word "girlfriend" hadn't escaped her ears either. She blinked at me twice.

"Well, I have to get back to my place and get a little rest. Keeping up with this girl is a full-time job in and of itself." Tom jerked his thumb at me, making Bea nod.

"You're preaching to the choir." She added, "Between the three of us, maybe we can manage to keep her out of trouble."

"You aren't helping." I snickered back.

"How about I come by your place tonight and bring you some chicken soup before I head off for the late shift? Crime never sleeps, you know," Tom asked in front of everyone. Full disclosure was his style, almost to a fault. But I couldn't help it. I kind of liked it. Tom made me the center of attention in a good way. I didn't feel he was ever talking down to me. We agreed on so many things. It was nice to feel that someone enjoyed me for exactly who I was. But for some reason I didn't like the idea of him coming over to bring me soup.

"I'm really pretty tired myself. After we close up, I think I'm just going to take a bath and go to bed." I wasn't lying. It was true. I was tired, and my body ached as if I'd gone ten rounds against Muhammad Ali.

"I understand." He rubbed my back. "Aunt Astrid, I'll be back tomorrow morning. Will you have a cup of coffee ready for me?"

"You know I will, Tom." She smiled and gushed over him. "You be careful out there." She waved with her good arm. The area the Rotmirage had scratched left three deep trenches of angry red gouges that had finally turned into dark-brown scabs.

Tom snuck one more kiss that was dangerously close to my lips before heading out the door, holding it open for none other than my favorite nemesis, Darla Castellan

.

Abusing Magic

Darla smiled at Tom, and I was surprised that he didn't check her out as she walked by. Instead, he just turned and walked on his way, peeking at me in the window and waving one last time.

As soon as male eye candy was gone, Darla went back to her obnoxious self.

"I'll have a green tea with lemon." She looked at Bea, Aunt Astrid, and finally at me. "My gosh, what happened to you all? Were you in a car accident or something?"

"Nope. A brawl broke out here at the café." I squinted my eyes like Clint Eastwood in *A Fistful of Dollars*. "We had to crack a few skulls. You should see the other guys."

"She's kidding, right?" Darla snickered at Bea. "No one understood your humor in high school. I don't know why you think anything has changed."

I chuckled. It was funny how the more tolerant I was toward Darla, the ruder she became. I thought I had just discovered my secret weapon. I hobbled behind the counter and cut a fresh lemon slice for the tea. Bea dropped the bag in the cup, and I added the lemon and hot water.

"On the house, Darla. It's always so nice to see you." I wiped my hands on my apron and smiled.

She looked at me as if I might have spit in her cup and she missed it while staring at me. With her cup in one hand and her designer purse in the other, she quickly took a seat next to the window so everyone could see her, pulled out her phone, and began scrolling through whatever was important to her. I'd bet there was an endless stream of selfies she hadn't admired in the past hour.

"So do you want to tell me why you turned down a visit from Officer Friendly, who was offering to bring you soup?" Bea slapped one hand on the counter and the other on her hip.

"I don't know," I murmured. "I really do just want to be alone tonight."

"Do you want me to check on you? I could bring

you some food," Bea said, pushing my hair behind my shoulder.

"What are you having?"

"Fried polenta with sautéed peppers and onions."

"Wow. No, thank you," I teased. "I've got food at my place. A couple of chili dogs sound good."

Bea wrinkled her nose but gave me a wink.

I just couldn't bring myself to talk about how I was feeling about Tom. After what he did for my family and me, there weren't words to describe it. And when a man and a woman don't have words to express themselves, sometimes they find other ways to do that, and I wasn't even remotely ready for that. I'll admit it. I was more scared of how I felt about Tom than of any Rotmirage or black-eyed kids or monsters underneath my bed. As crazy as it may seem, I wanted that feeling to last. This time, I was enjoying the mystery.

When it was quitting time, I bundled up as best I could and started to walk home. Walking down the sidewalk in the cold November air, I could smell the homes of the people who were burning firewood in their fireplaces.

Up in the sky was a bright crescent moon with half a dozen "witches' trails" across the sky. Those were actually exhaust trails from planes flying overhead. But I had heard a teenager call them that once, and it always struck me as kind of cute. A few stars twinkled, and I was pretty sure I could smell snow coming.

When I got to the door, my favorite face was there to greet me.

"Meow."

"Cold enough for you?" I asked as Treacle whipped his tail over the newspaper he was sitting on.

"Yes. But the hunts are better."

He meowed in the direction of the door, and I saw the small mouse he had brought for me. It was dead. Thinking of the poor creature in the attic of the Clare compound, I thought at least this mouse died for a natural purpose. Cats hunt. They eat some things, and they present other things as gifts to their owners.

"Well, that's a beauty," I said.

I scooped up the mouse in my one good hand and grabbed the newspaper with my wounded hand. Within seconds, Treacle and I were inside my house, engulfed in warmth and the familiar smell of sage and vanilla. I had yet to lose my scent from Aunt Astrid's aroma spell, so it had transferred onto all my clothes and furniture. There were worse things to smell like.

With the mouse dangling from its spindly tail between my fingers, I delicately laid it on a paper plate.

"I'll save this for later," I lied. I don't think Treacle knew I didn't really eat his gifts. He rubbed affectionately against my leg then went into the bedroom at a slow and satisfied stride and found his spot in the middle of my bed in order to catch up on some sleep.

I was about to wrap the dead mouse in newspaper, but the headline stopped me. *Wonder Falls Police Find Clares Dead in Separate Jail Cells.*

I read the article but could tell there was a ton of information that was being left out. Normally, I'd just dash over to my cousin's place and barge in, but it was so cold out tonight I thought I'd call first.

"Look outside your door," Bea said. I hurried and peeked through the little peephole to see both my aunt and Bea wrapped in scarves and coats, and I thought Aunt Astrid was wearing a quilt blanket around her shoulders. They had the newspaper, plus each was carrying a paper bag.

"We weren't sure if you had anything to eat," Bea teased as she began to unload her shopping bag with sliced veggies—*yuck*—and hummus. My aunt was much more organized and pulled out a batch of frozen lasagna that she quickly put in the oven.

"It that vegetarian lasagna?" I asked.

"Of course it is." Bea looked at me as if I had asked her if her hair was really red.

"I don't care. I'm hungry. I'll eat anything."

"Obviously," Aunt Astrid said, holding up the mouse on the paper plate.

"That was a gift from my prince." I nodded toward the bedroom. "He's now resting after a prosperous day of hunting mice." Taking the mouse on the plate, I unceremoniously dumped it in the trash and made sure it was covered completely. Then I spread out the newspaper, slapped my good hand right in the center of it, and sighed. "So? What do you think?"

My cousin actually admitted to feeling bad for the Clares.

"I hate to talk in these kinds of terms, but they really didn't have a choice."

After washing my hands, I grabbed a baby carrot and reluctantly chomped on it while I listened to Bea talk.

"They came from a long line of abusing magic, and it is only a matter of time before your mind can no longer see things correctly. It's really very sad." She shook her head.

"What did the paper say? I didn't read it." I chewed the carrot, which seemed to not get any smaller no matter how much I chomped on it.

Aunt Astrid went on to say that according to the papers, the Clares had refused to talk with their public defenders. They sat quietly in their separate cells, staring at the floor or the walls or the ceilings for hours. They wouldn't eat. By the time they were approved for suicide watch, it was too late.

"They were found hung by their bedsheets from the pipes across the ceilings." She pulled out a loaf of crusty Italian bread from her paper bag and tore off a piece, handing it to me. "Even though the holding cells have fifteen-foot-high ceilings and without the ability to fly, no man would be able to reach those pipes."

"How do you know that?" Bea asked.

We had all been to the police station where Jake worked. He gave us a private tour of the whole place, including the evidence room, the interrogation rooms, and the holding cells. But this was Tom's station on the other end of town. None of us had been there, or so we thought.

"That night, I went there to make sure these men were locked up tight."

"W-What?" I stuttered. Suddenly, my falling-through-the-ceiling story didn't seem nearly as cool as my aunt slipping into the police station unnoticed to spy on the latest inmates. I was almost jealous.

"I didn't want there to be a chance of them using any kind of magic or spell on any of the officers. These men manipulated their surroundings on a regular basis. They could make something ugly appear beautiful, something terrifying seem tranquil, something occupied seem suddenly empty." She tore into her own chunk of bread. "It was a good thing I arrived when I did."

Both Bea and I looked at each other in shock and simultaneously scooted our chairs in closer to listen.

"When I arrived, I watched as the two men were fingerprinted and photographed. I watched as they were each asked questions and without emotion admitted to killing Archie Jones, pushing him off the bridge after injecting him with the horse tranquilizer because he had somehow stumbled across their marijuana crop. They admitted to the murder of Calista Brown."

"Calista Brown? They said she committed suicide at the bridge, too." Bea shook her head.

"Apparently not. She was out exploring and bird watching when she stumbled onto their property. She saw the animals." Aunt Astrid pinched her lips together. "There were a few more names that I'm sure were all ruled suicides and contributed to the myth of Suicide Bridge and Evergrave Creek. But it was the Clares all along."

"So why did they admit to all this?" I asked, feeling a shiver as the obvious stared me in the face. Had the cavalry not arrived when it did, I might have been the next one hanging from Suicide Bridge.

"Without the protection of the Rotmirage, they could no longer continue. They were willing to give that thing whatever it wanted in order to keep living the way they did."

"But from what I saw, they lived like pigs." Bea wrinkled her nose and frowned.

"They saw it as a palace," Aunt Astrid stated.

"That's just plain weird," Bea muttered with a mouthful of broccoli and hummus.

"As things became more desperate and the reality of the situation was sinking in, they began to turn on each other. They were mumbling and hissing, and they weren't using our kind of words. But I could hear them."

"That's just plain creepy," I said, putting my good

hand to my chest.

"You have no idea," Aunt Astrid hissed.

Something had happened in those holding cells that more than disturbed Aunt Astrid. For an average person to look at her, she looked just as gentle and feminine as any woman in her early sixties. But Bea and I both knew what kind of spit and vinegar coursed through her veins when she was angry.

According to her, the Clares were cursing and screaming at each other like devils in Hades. To the police officers, it appeared they were barely moving around their cells, just managing to move to the bars then back to their metal beds. It was a mirage, like the one that covered up their marijuana plants. But in a slightly skewed dimensional level, they were tearing at their own skin, pounding against the walls, and digging at the floor below the bars. Being trapped was driving them mad.

"And they saw me there, wavering between dimensions, staying mostly hidden but peeking through for a few seconds here and there. They begged me to help them."

"That's interesting." My sarcasm was unavoidable. "They didn't like being in a cage? How ironic."

"You're reading my mind." Bea nudged me with her elbow.

Without engaging Otto or Leland Clare, Aunt Astrid conjured an enclosure spell. It wasn't your average binding spell.

"I tweaked it slightly to ensure that neither Otto nor Leland would try to escape. If they made any attempt to be in an environment that wasn't under lock and key, they would suffer debilitating stomach cramps. So if they weren't in a cell, if they weren't in handcuffs, if they weren't in a prison yard, they would not be able to function. It was quite brilliant, if I do say so myself. It's a shame they didn't live for me to see if it would actually work." Aunt Astrid popped a piece of bread in her mouth and chewed thoughtfully.

"So that's an ending I can live with," I said bitterly. "But if the ceilings were so high, how did they manage to get the sheets around the pipes to do themselves in?"

"I don't believe they did it to themselves." Aunt Astrid peeked at Bea and me from underneath heavy eyelids.

"You don't think the police did it!" Bea gasped.

"You don't think Tom would be part of something like that!" I almost chuckled at the idea, had my aunt not looked so grave.

"No." Aunt Astrid's voice was soft, but I couldn't

help feeling an icy edge to it. "I don't think for a minute that Tom had anything to do with it. But I can't say there wasn't a paranormal tint to everything."

I tossed my head to the right and let my mouth fall open.

"Are you saying you think someone or someones on the unincorporated Wonder Falls PD might be doing a little spell casting of their own?"

"I'm saying"—Aunt Astrid folded her arms over her chest—"that if the Clares came from such a long line of black-magic practitioners, it wouldn't surprise me if when they asked for help, this was the response."

Treacle decided to make an appearance and gave everyone's legs a good brushing as he slunk past before hopping up on my lap to continue his nap.

"Girls, this is why we have to guard what we know."

I don't think anything would make me shed a tear for the Clares. But as I watched my aunt, I saw a glimmer of sadness in her eyes.

"It can become such an overwhelming seduction to some people. Can you imagine what the Clares could have accomplished had they not abused their gifts?" She folded her hands. "It's such a waste."

"You've got a much bigger heart than me, Aunt Astrid." I set Treacle on the floor regardless of his purring protest and went to the oven to peek in on the lasagna, which was warming nicely. "I don't think they suffered nearly enough. Not after what I saw with those kittens and what Treacle told me from his friend Enzo." I snapped my fingers. "Do either one of you want to go with me tomorrow to check on them at Old Murray's?"

Bea had left the kittens with Marshmallow, Treacle, and Peanut Butter after she had made her way back home and called in backup. When we finished with all the excitement at the Clare farm, we took Enzo in as well. I had been in yesterday, and Enzo was still recuperating. The kittens had been adopted but were still being tended to. They'd move into their new home with Mrs. Bartlett, a wealthy widow in town who was good friends with Old Murray.

"The kittens are doing fine," Bea said then looked at her mother. "They are starting to play, and they're plumping up already."

"And Enzo?" Treacle and I had talked about inviting the stray to stay with us on an "as needed" basis. If he needed to stay, he could anytime.

But I wasn't stupid. I could tell by the look on my family's faces that the news wasn't good.

"Honey, we didn't really know how to tell you, but Enzo passed away in his sleep this morning." My aunt held her chin up and gave me a kind smile.

Treacle jumped back up on the table and looked at me.

I just let the tears come. I pulled my cat to me, holding him as if he were a baby over my shoulder, and I stroked his fur. He pushed his head into my chin and made not a single sound.

Bea had started to cry, too. It was never good to lose a familiar, especially in the line of duty, so to speak. But it was an inevitable part of life. At least Enzo didn't die locked up in a cage.

"Old Murray was with him the entire time. You know how he is about the animals," Bea said soothingly, wiping tears from her eyes. "He talked to Enzo and told him he'd see him at Rainbow Bridge. He said Enzo purred and purred until the very end."

I nodded. Treacle began to purr.

"Okay," I said trying to toughen up. "We can't save them all. Sorry to say."

"No, honey, we can't. But the ones we do usually end up saving us," Aunt Astrid said soothingly.

"And Enzo did that, literally," Bea added, smiling.

"He did." I said, squeezing the big black bundle of fur in my arms.

The One

✾

"I love the snow," I mused, looking out the sliding back door in Bea's kitchen.

"That isn't really snow." Jake leaned over my shoulder. "Those are called flurries. I don't mind those because I don't have to shovel them."

"I might invest in a snow blower this winter," I continued, thinking. "Maybe I'll ask Santa for one for Christmas."

"When are the rest of the guests going to arrive?" Aunt Astrid asked as she struggled with the leaf that went in the middle of Bea's dining room table to make it bigger.

"Blake should be here in about ten minutes," Jake answered and went over to the table to help.

"Tom will be by after his shift, and that should be in about half an hour." I sighed.

Normally, I enjoyed two Thanksgivings. There was the fun and exciting Thanksgiving at Bea's place where she made tofu turkey, mushroom stuffing, pureed cranberries, and a huge veggie salad. I'd politely take a taste of everything then pat my stomach and tell her it was delicious before I made my way back home to enjoy a real turkey submarine sandwich with all the fixings crammed between two thick pieces of bread that I picked up at Jimmy John's the previous day.

But this year was a little different. Since Tom was coming, Aunt Astrid offered to cook a real turkey instead of the traditional tofu.

"It isn't every year that we have a special guest like Tom joining us," Aunt Astrid said, chuckling. "We don't want him to think we are too weird. We'll ease him into it."

"I can't understand why anyone wouldn't like a tofu turkey." Bea huffed. "Tofu can be made to taste like anything you want it to."

"And that statement is enough to make me all the more suspicious of this chameleon sustenance called tofu." I bumped Bea with my hip as I began to help her in the kitchen. "Try the turkey," I whispered in her ear. "Come to the dark-meat side."

She laughed and bumped me back.

Just then, the doorbell rang, and Jake was off to get it. He had to be thankful for a little extra testosterone in the house.

We heard him happily greeting Blake and quickly jumping into some theory on a case they were working on or the score of a football game. It all sounded too masculine for me.

But when Blake entered into the room, I couldn't believe my eyes. He was not wearing the same all-business suit with wing tips that he usually did. Instead, he was wearing a casual pair of gray pants and a maroon-colored sweater. He looked relaxed and happy and very handsome.

"Blake, you know everyone," Jake said, "Let me get you something to drink."

Blake waved and walked immediately up to Aunt Astrid to give her a kiss on the cheek. What kind of perfume she wore to always attract the fellows, I didn't know, but whatever it was, the guys always sought her out first.

He went to Bea and gave her a hug and produced a card from his back pocket. They exchanged some pleasantries that I couldn't quite hear, but he said something that made her laugh.

Then it was my turn.

"Cath." He waved from across the counter.

That's it? That's all I get?

"Happy Thanksgiving, Blake. We're glad you made it." I felt as if I were grinning like Batman's arch nemesis, the Joker. My cheeks instantly ached.

I went back to helping with the salad, teasing Jake, and helping myself to the cornucopia of crackers, cheeses, cookies, and candies that Bea had spread out on the coffee table in the living room.

Peanut Butter, Marshmallow, and Treacle had all found their own special seats and were as much a part of the conversation as the rest of us were, even though they said very little but purred at every leg that passed by.

"You look really nice, Cath," Blake said quietly as I went to pour myself a glass of eggnog.

"Thank you, Blake. You look nice, too. I didn't think I would have recognized you without a suit on."

"Yeah, I thought maybe a change was in order."

I sipped the eggnog and looked around. Blake said nothing but didn't make any movements as though he wanted to leave.

"Can I get you a glass?" I offered. It seemed like the right thing to do.

"Sure," he replied.

I handed him an eggnog and raised my glass.

"A toast to the holidays." I smiled and blinked. "That everyone is with who they love."

He clinked his glass to mine, and I swore I saw the right corner of his mouth curl slightly. I thought it was a smile. I couldn't be sure. It was sort of like a Bigfoot sighting. It was there, and then it was gone. There was no way to be sure.

"What are your plans for the long weekend?" he asked, sounding as though he were in the interrogation room, questioning a witness.

"Well, since the café will be closed for the next two days, Aunt Astrid, Bea, and I will probably get it decorated for Christmastime. That's always like the first party of the season. Well, for me, it's the only party." I shuffled my feet nervously.

I was a little jealous of people who were married and got to go to several holiday parties with in-laws and different office parties and just those kinds of gatherings that they portray in chocolate or vodka commercials on television.

For me, it had been with my family. Not that I

didn't think that was great. I did. But like Blake and his casual wear, maybe a change was in order.

"That sounds like fun."

I nodded.

"How about you?" I asked nervously. I was starting to feel those old butterflies that used to come whenever I was around Blake. As if he were staring at me and seeing my slip or an exposed bra strap or something equally embarrassing.

"Well, I've actually got some time off coming to me." He stated it as if I'd never heard of a person taking time off work. Although I will admit hearing it from him was as odd as a nun carrying a surfboard.

"Really? Well, that will be nice. Are you travelling?"

"No. In fact, I was hoping that maybe you and I could talk." He took a step closer to me, making me crane my neck a little more to look up at him.

"We're talking right now." I didn't mean to be a smarty-pants. I just thought if he had anything to talk to me about, he had me right there.

"Yes, but I was hoping we could talk seriously, maybe over dinner somewhere."

I nearly choked on my eggnog. I didn't know what to say. Everything started moving in slow motion. I looked to my aunt and to Bea, but they were both busy talking amongst themselves, not paying any attention to me as I internally flailed my arms and screamed at the top of my lungs.

"I feel like I need to fix something with you." His eyes looked sad. "Something got broken."

"I didn't break anything." I held the crystal glass with the creamy liquid inside and turned it nervously in my hands.

"You didn't, Cath. You didn't at all. It's me, and I…"

Just as Blake was about to elaborate, the doorbell rang and Jake was off at a jog to get the door. A loud "Happy Thanksgiving!" came along with laughter and footsteps as Tom sauntered in. He was carrying several packages.

He made the rounds to everyone, presenting Bea with a beautiful planter of white poinsettias, and a bottle of some brown liquid to Jake, who smiled and thanked him. Of course, again, Aunt Astrid whistled her siren song, and Tom went running to give her a hug and kiss.

Before turning to me, he ambled up to Blake with his hand extended and a genuinely friendly smile on his face.

"Blake, how are you? Good to see you. But I've got to steal my girlfriend for just a second." I may as well have been standing there nude I blushed so hard. Tom took me by the hand and brought me toward the couch.

He kissed me on the cheek and handed me a card.

"Open it."

"Right here and now?" I looked around, but the only audience was Marshmallow and Peanut Butter. Treacle was busy rubbing against Tom's leg as if he were a scratching post.

"Yeah, its kind of important." He winked at me. I tore open the card and looked at the inscription.

"This looks like an invitation. A Christmas party?"

"The Wonder Falls police and fire stations have a huge Christmas bash every year. The guys wear tuxes. The girls wear their finest dresses. We get to dance and eat, and you'll get to meet everyone, and it is always a lot of fun."

"Wow."

"I've always gone stag. This is the first time I wanted to invite anyone. Would you go with me?" Tom took my hands in his. It was as if he'd asked me to wear his pin and go steady. I nodded yes.

But when I turned around and saw Blake standing there, I wondered if I should have. I had toasted that everyone be with the one they love.

About the Author

Harper Lin is the *USA TODAY* bestselling author of 6 cozy mystery series including *The Patisserie Mysteries* and *The Cape Bay Cafe Mysteries*.

When she's not reading or writing mysteries, she loves going to yoga classes, hiking, and hanging out with her family and friends.

www.HarperLin.com